I am your lover.
I am your death.
Pray for me.

COMMUNION
A chilling novel of faith—and murderous rage
by Frank Lauria

COMMUNION

by FRANK LAURIA

BANTAM BOOKS • TORONTO • NEW YORK • LONDON

COMMUNION
A Bantam Book / July 1977
2nd printing
3rd printing
4th printing
5th printing

For information address: Bantam Books, Inc.

ISBN 0-553-11241-4

Published simultaneously in the United States and Canada

PRINTED IN THE UNITED STATES OF AMERICA

For Elly S., Larry A., and Elly P.,
who made it happen
and to Ms. Ritvo and Mr. Sole, who
were there when the pages were blank.

And He took bread, and gave thanks and broke it, and gave it unto them saying, this is my body which is given for you: this do in remembrance of me.

Luke 22:19

1

It had been drizzling all afternoon, and the craggy Victorian houses huddled along the block had an ominous cast. Their stark turrets seemed threatening against the slate-gray sky; like spires on ancient, gloom-haunted castles.

When she'd been younger, Karen liked to pretend she was a fairy-tale princess in an evil city; on a mission to rescue her father, the king. But since she'd started studying for her First Communion, she'd been daydreaming about being a holy saint like St. Theresa, or Mother Cabrini; specially chosen by God to perform miracles on behalf of the sick and the poor.

Karen took a pink rubber ball from her raincoat pocket and absently bounced it against the wet sidewalk, imagining how she'd look in her communion dress. She saw herself in a shining white lace veil, approaching the altar to receive the sacred Host. As soon as she swallowed the wafer containing the body and blood of Christ, she'd be transformed by his grace into the purest, most beautiful saint in heaven. She'd float up to the clouds, Father Tom at her side.

Karen wondered if Father Tom knew how much she admired him. Sometimes at night . . .

The ball skidded off her fingers. As she retrieved it from the grimy puddle, Karen squeezed hard, trying to shut off her thoughts. It was a grave mortal sin to even think about liking a priest that way.

She quickly mumbled a Hail Mary and then began bouncing the ball, concentrating on keeping it in motion without a miss.

"K, my name is Karen, and my mother's name is Catherine . . . we live in Paterson, New Jersey, and my mother is a secretary. . . ." She chanted in a breathless singsong, completely unaware that she was being observed by a figure two stories above her—someone whose features were covered by a garishly tinted mask of a woman's smiling face.

✠ ✠ ✠

Alice Spages stood at the bedroom window, watching her sister through the slits in the mask, eyes narrowed by hate.

She envied Karen's natural grace and fair-skinned beauty that charmed everyone she met. But she despised Karen for stealing her father's love.

Alice always knew that her mother liked Karen best, but as long as Daddy was home, it didn't matter. When he divorced mother, everything crumbled like a sand castle. She was left without anyone.

Now Karen was using her goddamn First Communion to get everybody to be her slave, Alice fumed, teeth clenched behind the mask's fixed smile. She'd even called Daddy on the phone and weasled for a present, and yesterday it arrived. It was a lovely old-fashioned doll, with a real porcelain head that turned to show its three different faces. Mommy said it was real expensive.

And nothing for her at all—not even a card, Alice reflected bitterly, moving from the window.

A neon-pink flash caught Alice's eye, and she stopped to study her reflection in the mirror. The strange, smiling mask seemed almost real, she noted with satisfaction, as she zipped up her yellow slicker. With the hood pulled over her hair, nobody could tell who she was. Of course there was a St. Michael's emblem on her coat, but the entire school had the same raincoat.

The mask made her invisible.

Excited by the thought, she wandered to the toy baby carriage beside Karen's bed. Her sister's half of the room was a model of neatness, in sharp contrast to the clothes, magazines, and schoolbooks scattered around Alice's bed. Inside the carriage, a large doll was carefully propped up between two spotless pillows. It had silky blonde hair and blue eyes, just like Karen.

Without warning, Alice slapped the doll from its perch, then dug her fingers into its hair and savagely smashed its head against the side of the carriage. Unsatisfied, she pressed the pillow over the doll's beaming expression.

Suddenly Alice remembered something. She lifted her head and listened. Her breathing steamed loudly inside the mask, smothering all other sound.

Alice waited until she heard the familiar clatter of activity from the kitchen. She knew her mother was rushing to keep an appointment.

Reassured, she reached into her pocket for the matches. With ceremonial care, she pulled a match free and pressed it against the striker, poised to ignite destruction.

She lowered her hands inside the carriage, savoring the intoxicating mixture of anticipation and awe that flooded her brain.

"Alice!"

Her mother's muted shout jogged Alice from her reverie. She stuffed the matches in her coat as she hurried to Karen's bureau. She'd wasted too much time. There was something she needed to find before Mommy came looking for her.

Alice rummaged through the drawers until she found the cardboard box. Triumphantly, she unwrapped the tissue paper and extracted the doll her father had sent to Karen.

The doll's face was smiling. Alice gave the head a violent twist, and a new face appeared. This one was crying. There was a third face as well. She gave the head another rough turn, and it popped into place. The eyes were closed as if she were asleep. Or even dead.

"Alice!"

The shout was louder this time. She stuffed the doll inside her coat, removed the mask, and tiptoed out of the room. She continued down the corridor until reaching a partially open door. All she had to do was make it past the kitchen without being seen. She squinted through the crack and saw her mother bent over the table. With practiced ease, Alice stepped past the door and scampered soundlessly down the stairs.

Catherine Spages heard a faint click behind her and looked up expectantly, thinking it was Karen.

Except for the dim tinkle of music from the apartment below, the house was still.

She sighed and stepped into the hall. There wasn't much time. Sella's would be closed in less than an hour. If she didn't pick up the dress, Karen would never forgive her.

"Alice? Are you ready? We're leaving."

Catherine frowned at her reflection, as she buttoned her coat. At thirty-five, she had the creamy skin and trim, high-breasted figure of a twenty-year-old, but lately the responsibility of raising two children alone was starting to show. She looked tired, she decided. Typically, Dom paid the alimony and left her with the dirty work.

"Alice? Didn't you hear me call you?"

She gave her hair a final pat, picked up her purse, and headed for the children's bedroom.

It was empty.

Then Catherine remembered the click she'd heard a few minutes earlier. Alice had deliberately disobeyed orders and sneaked out.

Furious, she rushed to the window and saw Alice skipping across the street, two stories below.

"Alice, you come back here!" she yelled, struggling to open the window. It remained stuck, and she slapped the glass in frustration as Alice faded from sight.

"She's becoming more spiteful every day," Catherine muttered aloud as she hurried to the front door.

Halfway down the stairs, she met Karen.

Shocked by her daughter's hysterical tears and disheveled hair, Catherine grabbed her shoulders.

"What is it, baby? Are you hurt?"

"It's Alice, Mommy. She took it. She's going to break it. I had it all wrapped up and she took it," Karen sobbed.

"What did she take? Don't cry. You know I can't understand you when you cry."

Karen took a deep breath. "She took my doll. The doll Daddy sent me. She's going to break it—I know she is."

"No she won't, darling," Catherine soothed, dabbing her tears with a Kleenex. "I promise she won't break it. I'll take care of her. Calm down, baby. It's all right."

To her relief, Karen's sobbing trailed off.

"Now look, baby. I *have* to get to Sella's before they close. You want me to get your dress, don't you? And your veil?"

Karen nodded, trying to smile.

"That's my girl. Come on. Walk me outside. You can look for Alice while I pick up the dress. Tell her I want you right back home, or she'll be punished."

Although she was positive mere threats wouldn't frighten her sister, Karen knew better than to argue. If Mommy didn't pick up the dress on time, everything would be ruined. Her First Communion was on Sunday, and Sella's would be closed tomorrow.

When they reached the street, she kissed her mother good-bye, mounted her bicycle, and obediently rode off in search of Alice.

* * *

Before World War II, Paterson, New Jersey, flourished as the handmaiden of a thriving silk industry. By 1960, however, the era had been made obsolete by polyester, and abandoned mills threaded the residential areas like patches on an antique gown.

There was a condemned factory three blocks from Alice's house. She'd discovered a hole in the fence and for some months had been using the gutted building as her own private playground.

Alice headed directly for the old factory after leaving her house, pausing every block to make sure she wasn't followed. She had to get to the sanctuary before Karen found her.

She was almost there when a rainbow streak of color in the window of a candy store attracted her attention. As she studied the variety of grotesque masks strung across the glass, Alice immediately regretted having left her own disguise at home. She needed it to make herself invisible. Biting her lip, she scanned the gaudy monsters and clowns without interest until she spotted the woman's face in the corner. Made from transparent pink plastic with slanted eyes and smiling, heart-shaped lips, it was exactly like the one she'd left behind.

She squinted at the tag taped to the mask's chin. It read: *Jackie Kennedy 49¢.*

As her fingers closed on the two quarters in her pocket, Alice smiled back at the pretty lady above her.

* * *

Karen was just about to turn back for home when she spotted the girl in a yellow St. Michael's raincoat on the next block. Sure it was Alice, she pedaled faster as the girl ran to the corner and ducked out of sight.

By the time Karen reached the corner, the street was empty. It was raining harder, but she cruised past the boarded-up mills, determined to bring Alice home.

A glimpse of movement caused her to brake quickly, and she turned in time to see the girl entering an old factory. The building was surrounded by a cyclone fence, and it took Karen a few minutes to find a way through.

"Alice! Come out!" she shouted, as she approached the crumbling structure. She saw an open door and hesitated, suddenly aware that it was dusk and night was closing fast.

Then a yellow blur moved past the door.

"Mommy says to come home," Karen called, stepping into the musty factory. She peered across the rubbled floor, unwilling to go further.

"Alice?"

A face floated out of the shadows, grinning like a succubus.

Karen whirled to run but her way was blocked by the small, eerie figure in a bright yellow slicker. Even though she realized it was Alice behind the mask, she shrank back in panic.

"Where's my doll?" she demanded, trying to maintain her courage.

"You'll never know," Alice mocked, her voice muffled by the mask.

"What did I ever do to you? Why are you being so mean?"

Alice shrugged. "I don't have your old doll. Go away! You don't belong here!"

"You do so have it. You showed it to me before. In front of the house. Give it back or I'll tell Mommy."

"If you tell Mommy anything, you'll never see that doll again."

The steely edge in her calm tone frightened Karen. Although Alice was only a year older, she was much stronger physically, and completely ruthless. Karen knew from experience that her sister never forgave before extracting revenge.

With a sudden lunge, she pushed past Alice and ran outside. The cold rain seemed to dissolve her fear. She mounted her bike and looked back at the shadowy doorway.

"Come on out if you're so brave," she challenged.

There was no answer, but Karen knew that Alice was listening, somewhere in the darkness.

She turned her bike around and pedaled slowly to the street.

"Mommy's bringing my communion dress and

veil," she shouted triumphantly over her shoulder. "And if you don't get home soon, you'll really be punished."

The only response was a bolt of lightning that cracked the sky like an egg.

2

Although annoyed that the girls still hadn't returned, Catherine felt a glow of satisfaction when she deposited the cardboard box containing Karen's dress on the table. At last her job was finished. She'd done everything possible for her daughter's First Communion, from coaching her cathechism lessons to taking care of last-minute alterations on the dress. Now it was up to Karen.

She had every confidence that her daughter would take the sacred event in stride. Karen had a sense of responsibility that was rare in young girls these days, Catherine reflected proudly. If only Alice would follow her example, life might become much simpler. That child was becoming downright delinquent. Twice this term she'd been called to St. Michael's Parochial School because of Alice's unruly behavior.

She'd been lenient, understanding that the divorce might have left emotional scars, but couldn't ignore the blatant disobedience much longer. Right after Karen's communion, she'd have a long, serious talk with Alice. Perhaps even make arrangements for professional help.

She put the teapot on to boil and glanced at the clock. Where could they be at this hour? Then she heard the front door open.

"It's me," Karen called.

"Is your sister with you?"

Karen burst into the kitchen. "Where is it? Did you get it?"

"Don't worry, it's here. Where's Alice?"

"She's coming. Can I see it? Pretty please?"

"You're soaked," Catherine admonished. "Get out of those wet things and dry your hair first."

"Just let me see it. I'll be careful—I promise."

"All right. The box is in the dining room. But don't wrinkle the dress when you take it out."

Catherine smiled as she stacked the dinner dishes and listened to the delighted exclamations in the next room.

"Oh, it's just perfect. I can't wait for Sunday."

At the sound of the front door slamming shut, Catherine's smile faded.

"Alice? Where have you been?"

Receiving no answer, she turned and saw Alice standing in the doorway. Her flat features were set in a defiant scowl, the wet strands of hair framing her fish-eyed glare like seaweed.

"Listen, Miss Independence, it's a good thing you decided to come home," Catherine scolded. "Don't think you'll get away with this. I won't tolerate deliberate disobedience. Now tell me this minute. Where have you been going these days?"

She was interrupted by the whistle of the teakettle. "Take off those wet things!" she snapped, turning to the stove. "We'll settle this later."

Alice ignored the instructions and walked into

the dining room where Karen was prancing happily, dress held aloft like a banner.

Seeing the veil, Alice snatched it off the table and ran to the mirror. She pressed the lacy white fabric to her rain-matted hair, grimacing at her reflection. Not even the veil could make her pretty.

"Mommy, she's making it wet! Make her take it off!"

When Catherine entered the dining room, Karen was leaning against the table, face screwed up in frustration. A few feet away, oblivious to her sister's shouts, Alice sullenly modeled the communion veil at the mirror, like some homely, unwilling bride.

For a moment Catherine was torn between anger and pity. It wasn't easy for Alice. She was going through an awkward stage. And it was painfully apparent that she lacked Karen's natural beauty.

"Mommy, make her take it off!"

Catherine's patience crumbled under the pressure of whining children, nagging responsibilities, and a dinner about to burn.

"Take that veil off right now!" she screamed. "Do you hear? Where have you been going these afternoons? Don't think I haven't noticed!"

Alice turned, features wrinkling like a vindictive crone. "What do you care where I go? I'm not Karen. Take your veil—I don't want the stupid thing anyway! I hate all of you." She threw the veil to the floor and dashed into the corridor.

Catherine followed, but by the time she reached the bedroom, it was locked. Exasperated, she pounded on the door. "Open this instant! What's wrong with you, Alice? Why are you being so horrid to your sister?"

"She's not my sister! Leave me alone!"

The muffled reply punctured Catherine's anger

and touched a profound maternal instinct. Fists clenched helplessly, she stared at the door, thoughts battered by confusion and guilt. Perhaps she'd been neglecting Alice these days.

"Oh, Mommy, it's ruined."

Karen's wail pulled her from the door. Just two more days, she promised. Right after Karen's First Communion, she'd make a special effort to find out what was troubling Alice.

Karen was sitting on the floor, sobbing uncontrollably, the veil clutched against her chest.

"She got my veil all wet . . . it's ruined," she stammered.

Overcome by a rush of compassion, Catherine knelt and embraced her daughter. It wasn't fair, she thought, rocking Karen gently. Someone so good and lovely shouldn't be made to suffer like this.

"It's all right, baby," she crooned. "Don't cry. Mommy will fix it—I promise." She tugged the veil free and examined it. "See? There's nothing wrong with it. I'll iron it right away."

"Why is she so mean?" Karen moaned. "I hate her . . . I just . . ."

Catherine tenderly covered Karen's mouth with her hand. "Now, now," she whispered. "Remember, she's your sister. You don't want to commit a sin before your First Communion, do you?"

To distract her, Catherine arranged the veil on her hair. "I can fix it. See, nothing happened to it. You look just like a little bride."

Karen tried to smile, taken by the reflection of her own loveliness in her mother's face.

"There—that's it. Smile, baby," Catherine said, hugging her tight. "I could just squeeze you to death. I think you're going to be the prettiest one there. Wait till Father Tom sees you. And don't forget he wants us to visit him tomorrow, right after confession."

The reminder evaporated Karen's misery. "Oh, I can't wait," she confided, eyes shining. "Besides you and Daddy, Father Tom is the most wonderful person in the whole world!"

Her enthusiasm aroused conflicting emotions in Catherine. Since becoming pastor of St. Michael's parish, Tom had proved to be a vital force in the community. He had a special knack with children, and they all adored him. Especially Karen.

"Then be a good girl and change clothes," she said firmly. "You don't want to catch cold now."

Karen gave her a loud kiss. "I love you, Mommy. Thanks."

Still preoccupied, Catherine pulled the ironing board from its niche. Even though she'd known Tom since high school, she sometimes felt she didn't know him at all. Since taking his vows, he seemed almost possessed with inspired purpose. He hadn't always been as dedicated, however.

Catherine remembered their student days when Dominic and Tom were the school basketball stars and she was a cheerleader.

It was always the three of them, through those years. Dominic Spages, Tom Hale, and Catherine trailing along.

Dominic was the serious one then, intent on succeeding at whatever he attempted; while Tom was fun-loving, and slightly reckless.

Tom was inordinately fond of practical jokes, such as filling all the tubas in the school band with soapy water before the Thanksgiving concert.

That one cost him a whole season's suspension from the basketball team, and St. Michael's lost the city cup to Eastside High School. It was only Dominic's pleading and Tom's fine academic record that prevented his being expelled from the strict parochial school.

Dominic and Tom seemed to balance each other, and the two of them were inseparable. Even though Catherine was technically Dominic's steady girl, she sometimes wondered which of them she really preferred as a prospective husband. But time and Tom's decision settled that question at graduation.

Without any warning, Tom announced that he was entering the seminary, to study for the priesthood. At first they'd thought it was another practical joke, but it soon became clear he was serious this time.

Dominic went on to Columbia University, and she'd found a job with a local law office. They'd married during Dominic's third year and Alice was born before he graduated. It was a struggle, but it was also the best phase of their marriage. They'd needed each other then, and they spent months alone together while Dom prepared for his finals.

Dominic was extremely ambitious, however, and after graduation he put all his energies into making his student dreams come true.

And they did. For him.

Dominic was the fair-haired boy of Madison Avenue, but their marriage was already past its prime.

There were fights, and then the long silence. Dominic wanted to leave Paterson for a house in a fashionable suburb; he cultivated strange new friends and spent weeks away on business trips.

The divorce came as no surprise, but it still hurt her deeply. As a Catholic, she'd never really considered the possibility. She'd been raised to believe that marriage was an indissoluble sacrament.

The first few years had been extremely difficult, until Tom returned to St. Michael's as its pastor. It was his friendship and wisdom that finally helped her recover the lost threads of her life.

Although relieved that her daughter had the

good sense to choose someone like Father Tom Hale as a hero, Catherine was aware of the possible complications.

After all, Karen wasn't exactly a child. The divorce had delayed her religious training, and she was the oldest girl in the class.

Catherine had known Tom since their school days and shared Karen's admiration. But it worried her a bit. A young girl could easily develop a romantic crush on a young priest who had the looks of a film star, the charm of a diplomat, and the spiritual intensity of a saint.

She still recalled the day he'd taken her aside after mass, to report on Karen's wonderful progress, and to tell Catherine that her daughter had been chosen as candle bearer for the communion class.

When she tried to express her gratitude, he'd modestly brushed away her thanks.

"Karen's the product of her mother's devotion and faith, Kay," he explained, as he escorted her to the entrance. "You should be proud—that's what I really wanted to say."

It was just a simple thing, but he made it seem like the vision at Fatima. She could still hear his vibrant tone and feel the warmth of his fingers on her arm.

A wave of shame washed the memory away, followed immediately by a grim tide of determination.

Starting next Monday, Catherine resolved, her daughters were going to learn that life wasn't all fancy frills.

✠ ✠ ✠

Father Tom stroked the cleft in his chin, unable to decide where to hide the small package. He hefted the tiny ribboned box in his hand, speculation lining his rugged features as he paced back and forth.

A buzz at the front door settled his problem. He tucked the package behind a bowl of fruit on the sideboard and then strolled to the vestibule.

At the second buzz, he quickened his pace, wondering why Mrs. Tredoni hadn't answered. As he passed the kitchen, he saw her impassively mopping the floor.

"Didn't you hear the bell?" he asked mildly.

Mrs. Tredoni didn't look up from her work. "Are your guests so important they can't wait a minute?" she droned. "Are they more important than keeping this rectory clean for you?"

"And very clean it is, too," Father Tom agreed genially. "I'll get the door. But when you get time, I'd appreciate some of that delicious cake you made. And I'm sure our guests would as well."

As expected, Catherine Spages was at the door with Karen and Alice. He tried to keep his expression blank as they exchanged greetings, but Karen wasn't fooled a bit.

"You look like the Cheshire cat, Father Tom," she teased.

"Me? How so?"

"You have this funny little smile. Like you have a secret."

"Secret? Me?" He glanced at Catherine. "Do you know what she's talking about?"

"I'm always the last to hear everything," she laughed. "It's a mother's lot."

"My surprise," Karen blurted. "Don't you have a surprise for me, Father Tom?"

"Really, Karen, that's rude," her mother chided.

"It's my fault," Tom said, patting Karen's shoulder. "I promised her something special if she studied hard for her First Communion. And she's been my best pupil." He beamed down at her. "Just be patient—okay?"

The members of St. Michael's parish were blue-collar workers with conservative views, and the church rectory reflected their basic distrust of extravagance. The three-story house was badly in need of repair, and the cramped, drafty rooms were furnished with secondhand pieces, donated over the years.

To Karen, however, the rectory seemed as grandiose as a cathedral. It was the place where Father Tom carried out his holy work.

Trying to suppress her anticipation, she sat beside her mother at the table and clasped her hands.

Father Tom gave her a stern look. "Well, now, little lady, do you know what day it is today?"

"Today is Saturday."

"Yes, but what else?"

Momentarily flustered, Karen glanced at her mother. Then it dawned.

"Today was my first confession," she declared triumphantly.

"Exactly right," Tom congratulated. "Even though your First Communion is a big event in your life, the sacrament of confession is just as important. For that reason I hope you made a good confession today."

"Oh, yes, Father Tom," Karen exclaimed as Mrs. Tredoni entered carrying a large tray. Her haggard, hawk-featured face remained expressionless as she served the cake and tea.

"And here's your surprise," Tom announced grandly. "Chocolate cake made by Mrs. Tredoni herself. What do you say to that, Karen?"

Struggling unsuccessfully to overcome her disappointment, Karen managed a weak smile.

"Thanks, Mrs. Tredoni."

"It was Father's request," the housekeeper sniffed, her tight-lipped frown making it clear that she had enough to do without catering to spoiled children.

"I don't know how to express my own thanks for the way you've looked after Karen," Catherine said as Mrs. Tredoni departed.

The priest shook his head. "I should be thanking you, Kay. She's been a real inspiration to the entire class. And to me as well."

Unnoticed by the others, Alice left the table and began wandering aimlessly around the dining room. She was sick of hearing about Karen's virtues and longed to be in her own sanctuary.

"Aren't you going to have some cake, Alice?" Father Tom called.

She spun, fists clenched. "I'm not hungry."

The savage suspicion in her sullen expression warned the priest to let the matter drop. This was Karen's treat, and he didn't want it marred by an outburst of sibling rivalry.

"Ummm, this cake is delicious," Catherine said. "How about you, Tom? Are you fasting?"

He grinned sheepishly. "With Mrs. Tredoni's cooking, it's a battle to keep my weight down."

"You gotta have faith," she admonished with mock gruffness. "How many times have I told you, faith can do anything."

"Sure . . . it's easy for you to say," Father Tom countered, "but I don't want to be the mountain that faith moves."

Temporarily ignored during their playful bantering, Alice slipped into the corridor and walked slowly through the strange house, pretending she was a burglar.

A rasping sound drew her to a half-open door. Just outside, she paused and took the mask from her pocket.

The moment she placed the grinning pink face over her own features, she felt secure. She was invisible again, and nobody could hurt her.

She carefully leaned inside and saw the old

priest sitting in a wheelchair. He was asleep and the rasping sound she'd heard were snores.

Alice backed away from the door and tiptoed to the other end of the hall. She turned a corner and froze.

Someone was kneeling on the floor, just outside Father Tom's dining room. For long seconds she remained motionless, unsure of what to do; listening to the voices filtering into the silent corridor.

"A little bird told me, Karen, that you're the prettiest girl in the class," Father Tom confided. "All those boys talking about you, and here I thought I was your best beau."

"Oh, Father, that's against church law," Karen giggled.

Alice took a tentative step back and the floor creaked.

Mrs. Tredoni turned. When she saw the masked child behind her, the blood dropped from her face and she crossed herself.

"Who's there?" she quavered, lifting her scrub brush like a weapon. "Who is it?"

A moment later she scrambled to her feet and was swooping down on Alice like an avenging angel, sharp features twisted in anger.

"Oh, you horrid child! Get out of here!" she croaked. "Get out!"

Panicked, Alice dodged around her and ran to the safety of the dining room.

"Take that thing off your face!" Catherine shouted as Alice rushed inside. She turned to the housekeeper standing at the door, brush still raised. "I'm sorry, Mrs. Tredoni."

Alice pulled off the mask and glared at her mother.

"Who gave you permission to roam?" Catherine demanded. "Stay in here with us and try to remember you're a young lady. What will Father Tom think of you? You probably frightened Mrs. Tredoni half to death!"

"Now, now, Kay. I'm sure she didn't mean it. She's just a child." Tom chuckled. "It was just a little joke, wasn't it, Alice?"

Alice stared at the floor, unwilling to answer. He didn't fool her. He hated her like all the rest. All he cared about was his precious Karen.

"How about some cake?" Father Tom suggested. "Still plenty left."

Wordlessly, she stalked to the far side of the table and sat down.

"I just don't understand what gets into her," Catherine murmured apologetically.

"Just a stage," he reassured. "She'll grow out of it. We did, didn't we?"

He winked at Alice, then leaned closer to Karen. "Come to think of it, I seem to recall that there's something else around here for you besides Mrs. Tredoni's cake." He tapped his forehead in mock concentration. "Let me see now . . . where did I put it . . .

"Oh, yes." He went to the sideboard, and extracted the package from behind the fruit bowl. "Yes, I think this is it."

Karen reached for the package, then paused, hands fluttering shyly.

"Go on, take it," Father Tom coaxed. "It's got to be yours. There's no other Karen Spages around here, is there?"

She took the gift, then paused again, glancing from the package to her mother.

"Open it," Father Tom said. "We all want to see what it is."

Karen eagerly tore the wrapping from her gift. There was a red velvet box inside. She opened the box and took out an antique gold crucifix on a thin gold chain.

"Look, Mommy," Karen exclaimed, eyes dancing with joy. "Isn't it beautiful?" She left her chair and dangled the crucifix in front of Alice. "Look what Father Tom gave me," she said breathlessly. "Isn't it the most beautiful cross you ever saw?"

"It belonged to my mother," Father Tom said softly.

Catherine's smile faded. "Tom, you shouldn't have! What if she loses it?"

"Who else would I give it to, Kay?"

Catherine shrugged, both moved and embarrassed by the mild question.

Trembling with suppressed hatred, Alice was unable to take her gaze from the carved, gleaming crucifix in her sister's hand. Through the seething turmoil in her brain, one thought burned like a beacon. She'd make them all pay for the way they treated her—even if she went to hell!

Catherine looked up.

"Karen, what do you say to Father Tom?"

"She doesn't have to say anything," Father Tom grinned. "But she can give me a great big kiss."

As Karen hurried to comply, Alice noticed a small table behind her chair. It was adorned with glass figurines and covered by a lace doily. The edge of the doily seemed to be only an arm's length away. She reached back and tugged at the doily, slowly drawing the figurines closer to the edge.

"I love you, Father Tom," Karen was saying. "I really love you."

The priest stroked her hair. "I know you'll take good care of it. I've always . . ."

The loud crash interrupted him.

Catherine whirled and saw Alice backing away from the broken glass strewn near her chair.

"What have you done?" she yelled.

"I didn't mean it, Mommy, I couldn't help it!"

Alice shouted, fists clenched. "I didn't mean it!"

✣ ✣ ✣

All through dinner, Karen tried to coax Alice out of her sullen mood.

Karen understood that her sister resented the presents and attention she was getting, and she also knew why. So, she made a special effort to help Alice feel better.

"You can have the last piece of apple pie," Karen smiled, offering her sister the plate.

Alice made a face. "Eat it yourself! I don't want anything from you!"

Catherine couldn't understand her daughter's behavior, and she refused to tolerate it any longer. She grabbed Alice's wrist as the child jumped up and held it firmly.

"Just a minute, young lady. I haven't given you permission to leave the table. And I won't until you apologize to your sister."

Alice glowered and shrank back.

"Why are you being so mean to your sister?" Catherine persisted, softening her tone. "We should all be a family."

"I'm not part of this family!"

The flat declaration stung Catherine's emotions. "Don't say that, please," she whispered. "It's not fair."

"It's not fair that Karen is having her First Communion before me," Alice blurted. "I'm the oldest."

Catherine sighed, struggling for patience. "Now, you know you can't blame Karen for that. Things got mixed up after Daddy left, and you didn't study hard enough. But if you memorize your lessons and learn to behave in class, you'll be taking your First Communion with the next group."

Sensing that her outburst had touched her mother's sympathy, Alice pressed her advantage.

"I didn't get any presents!" she muttered. "Karen gets everything."

"Please don't feel that way," Catherine said soothingly. "Tell you what. If you promise to study extra hard and tell your sister you're sorry, next week we'll see about that radio you wanted."

"That will be wonderful," Karen said, extending her hand to Alice. "And it's okay—you don't have to say you're sorry or anything."

"There—you see?" Catherine beamed. "Can you understand that we love you?"

Alice's expression was blank as she nodded.

"That's my girl." Catherine gently tugged Alice's limp hand closer to Karen's. "Now promise you'll try to be friends."

Seeing the antique crucifix dangling from her sister's neck renewed Alice's anger, but she repressed the urge to throw another tantrum. She'd gotten enough for now. She reached across the table and clasped Karen's hand.

"I promise," she mumbled. "And I'm sorry."

"I'm so glad you said that," Catherine exclaimed, hugging her tight.

In her enthusiasm, she didn't notice that Alice had her other hand behind her back, with two fingers tightly crossed.

✢ ✢ ✢

Alice was up early the next morning, anxious to leave the house before everyone started fussing. She was washed, dressed, and almost out the door when her mother spotted her.

"Just where do you think you're going? Today is Karen's First Communion—or have you forgotten?"

"I'm just going out for a little while. I'll be at church in time. I promise."

"Make sure you do, or you'll be sorry," Catherine warned.

Alice scampered out the door before her mother could change her mind. There was something important she had to do before going to church.

Mentally reviewing each detail of her plan, she descended the stairs. At the second landing a hoarse wheeze interrupted her calculations. It was Alphonso, their neighbor, standing at the door of his apartment.

His loose-fleshed bulk filled the space like a heap of quivering gray Jell-O; bald head a tiny grape on the massive body that weighed well over four hundred pounds.

He leered at her, wet lips pursed as he stroked the kitten curled against his soiled undershirt. "Where are you going?"

Alice stared at him with contempt. "None of your business, fatso."

"I'll give you a dollar if you go to the store for me," he whined. "They won't deliver on Sunday."

Without answering, Alice moved to the stairs.

"I'm too sick to go myself," Alphonso wheezed after her. "Please. Please."

When he heard the front door slam shut, he shuffled back into a living room littered with newspapers, empty food cans, and large cardboard boxes. The boxes were for his eleven cats.

Gasping from the exertion of moving his immense mass, he perched on a sagging couch and began spooning cat food into a bowl.

"That little bitch!" he told the cats gathering around him. "I'm going to get that little slut—don't you worry."

A dab of meat stuck to his urine-stained trousers. Before the nearest cat could reach it, Alphonso's finger scooped it up and popped it into his mouth.

"She hates us, my little pussies," he went on. "But I'll fix her. I have ways—oh, yes!"

Pensively smacking his lips, he placed a 78 record on a battered phonograph nearby. As the strains of *Madame Butterfly* floated across the filthy room, he leaned back and closed his eyes.

✢ ✢ ✢

Erected in the twenties by immigrant craftsmen who took an Old World pride in their work, St. Michael's church boasted a mosaic of the Last Supper in its spacious lobby, and imported marble pillars in its high-domed interior.

Catherine stood outside, nervously twisting her white gloves as she scanned the street. If Alice broke her word today, it was the last straw, she decided angrily. The child lied to her—she deliberately intended to be late.

There were still a few people arriving, but she could hear the organ music inside, signaling the start of the mass.

Karen darted out of the lobby, face stricken with anxiety. "I can't find her anywhere, Mommy. She's not inside. I'll be late."

"It's all right," Catherine soothed. "I'll take care of everything. Don't worry about Alice."

She straightened her daughter's veil and stepped back. With the white lace framing her delicate features and Tom's antique crucifix around her neck, Karen looked like a Renaissance madonna.

"Aunt Kate, Aunt Kate—Sister Felicia wants Karen right away," a plump girl blared from the entrance.

Catherine gave her daughter a quick kiss.

"Okay, join your group. I'll be there in a minute."

Karen hesitated. "But Mommy, you might miss . . ."

The girl ran over and took Karen's hand. "Come on," she nagged. "They're almost ready."

Catherine forced a smile at her overfed, hypertense niece. "I won't miss a thing—I promise."

She continued pacing fretfully for a few more minutes after Angela escorted Karen inside. The possibility of an accident crossed Catherine's mind, but was angrily dismissed by the reminder that Alice's absence was part of a vicious pattern. The child was simply unmanageable.

The mass had begun when she finally gave up and entered the church. The choir in the balcony was singing the salutation as Father Tom stood at the base of the altar, intoning the prayers.

Every pew was packed with proud parents and it took some searching before Catherine found a place in one of the front rows. Too late she saw that her older sister, Annie, was sitting in the row just behind, with her husband Jim and their son Robert.

Annie's self-righteous meddling never failed to upset her. Telling herself to stay calm, Catherine genuflected and slipped into the pew. The moment she was seated, Annie leaned forward.

"Where's Alice?" she hissed.

Catherine shrugged and put a finger to her lips.

Ruffled, Annie glared accusingly at the bald, rumpled man beside her. Jim Lorenzi shifted uncomfortably on the wooden bench, wondering how he'd offended his wife this time, and what it would cost to appease her.

✠ ✠ ✠

The large storeroom at the rear of the church was a turmoil of youthful energy.

Boys in dark blue suits, white carnations and

white armbands, milled about restlessly under the watchful eye of Sister Felicia. On the other side of the room, the girls huddled in small, whispering groups, fussing with their starched white veils.

Sister Felicia clapped her hands briskly when she heard the choir. "Everyone in place. Remember your instructions: keep at least three feet apart from the pair ahead of you."

She opened the door and signaled a nun stationed at the main aisle. "First pair step up," she commanded.

The first boy and girl on each line approached the doorway.

"Go to the confessional and stop right there," Sister Felicia ordered, pointing to the arched, curtained booth a short distance away. "Don't move until you're told."

As the first pair slowly walked to the confessional, Sister Felicia motioned for the next two, until soon there was a double line, spaced three feet apart, strung from the middle of the room to the confessional; girls on one side, boys on the other.

At the altar, Father Tom completed the ritual sacrifice of the mass and lifted the gold chalice.

The choir began to sing as Sister Felicia moved ahead and herded the children towards the altar.

Karen was the last to leave the large room. She didn't have a partner. It was her solemn task to follow the class down the center of the aisle, holding the big white candle.

Cupping the wavering flame with one hand, she moved through the door. She wanted to see Father Tom but her view was blocked by the pillars. She wondered if he'd notice the crucifix, then scolded herself for being so presumptuous. Father Tom would be inspired by the body and blood of Christ when he gave them communion.

Still intent on keeping the thick, heavy candle

properly lit, she paused beside the confessional and waited for the pair ahead to shuffle to the center aisle and complete their genuflections.

The candle was yanked away so quickly that her first fear was for the flame.

Then she felt it crushing her throat, cutting off her surprised cry as she was jerked into the confessional booth. The darkness made it all seem unreal. She was being swallowed by agonizing waves of pressure that battered relentlessly at her lungs. It had to stop now. She screamed, spinning faster into the tumultuous blackness. The pain had to stop.

But no one heard her, and it didn't stop.

By the time the death panic pierced her confusion, all her strength was fading into the feverish roar filling her skull. She kicked wildly as the howling agony ballooned against her ribs until it burst, hurling her into infinite silence.

The choir's joyous hymn drowned out the hoarse gasps of the small figure who emerged from the curtained booth dressed in a yellow St. Michael's slicker. Face obscured by the upraised hood and hidden from view by the pillars, the figure dragged Karen's body along the marble floor to the storeroom.

Once inside, she closed the door and pulled the body to a wooden chest.

Minutes later, still panting heavily from the exertion of stuffing the body inside the chest, she carefully wrapped Karen's arms around the large candle.

The crimson lips on the mask covering the figure's face were fixed in a cupid smile as she took the matches from her coat and lit the candle.

After pausing a few seconds to watch the flame crawl across the white dress, she reached down and tore the crucifix from Karen's bruised, lifeless throat.

3

A pleasant tingle of anticipation dispersed Catherine's anxiety when she saw the children coming down the aisle.

Heads bowed, they slowly filed past the admiring parents and relatives, jamming the center pews. When they reached the altar, they moved forward in pairs, like miniature brides and grooms, to kneel at the rail and receive the sacrament.

Catherine waited impatiently as each pair shuffled past, straining for a glimpse of her daughter.

Annie tapped her shoulder. "Where's Karen?"

"There's the last pair," Jim added. "Still don't see her."

Catherine frowned at her brother-in-law.

"Be patient," she snapped. "She'll be along. She was chosen to carry the candle."

But as she looked back at the empty aisle, her anger was smothered by a vague apprehension.

Sister Felicia was worried as well.

Face clamped in a bulldog scowl, she waddled swiftly to the rear of the church in search of Karen.

Then she stopped, bulbous nose twitching at a strangely pungent odor. A moment later, she saw the fumes drifting from the storeroom and rushed inside. The room was filled with acrid smoke that gushed from a burning chest.

Unruffled, she threw open a window, located the extinguisher, and began spraying the chest. As the smoke abated, she realized the fire came from inside and used the extinguisher to pry back the lid.

The shriveled, blistered mass of sizzling flesh seemed to erupt from the chest.

Sister Felicia dropped the extinguisher and staggered to the door, fighting back a surge of nausea.

"Fire!" She screamed hysterically, unable to comprehend what she'd seen.

✠ ✠ ✠

Father Tom was unaware of any disturbance until he noticed the odd behavior of his altar boy.

It was the boy's job to hold the paten underneath the chin of each child who received communion. The brass plate was used to catch the sacred wafer if it fell from the supplicant's outstretched tongue.

When Tom moved to the next child, however, the paten wasn't in place.

Instead, the altar boy was gazing toward the back of the church. Tom heard a faint shout from that direction but was more concerned with the girl at the rail, waiting for the Host.

Father Tom's nudge recaptured the altar boy's attention, and he lifted the paten sheepishly. *"Corpus Domini Jesu Christi,"* Father Tom mumbled, making the sign of the cross with the wafer. *"Custodiat animam tuam in vitam eternam. Amen."*

After placing the wafer on the girl's outstretched tongue, Father Tom automatically moved to the next child kneeling at the rail.

His consecrated fingers dipped into the chalice and he began the prayer anew, ignoring the rising commotion among the congregation. The girl in the yellow coat was the last one at the communion rail, and he wanted to complete the most important phase of the mass before . . .

Then it struck him.

The child kneeling before him was wearing a St. Michael's raincoat instead of a veil. Because her eyes were closed and her tongue extended, it took Father Tom a confused moment to recognize Karen's sister. Alice Spages.

But Alice hadn't made her first confession. What she was doing was a serious mortal sin. Dazed by the sheer brazenness of her attempt, Tom withdrew the wafer and replaced it in the chalice.

"Fire!" a woman screamed. "There's a fire."

Alice's eyes sprang open.

They blazed with defiance as she stared at Father Tom, stubby features hardened by a sullen intensity that made her seem strangely old.

Wordlessly, she backed away from the altar rail and lost herself in the crowd jamming the center aisle.

✠ ✠ ✠

"My God, where's Angela?" Annie was yelling above the noise.

Blindly following her sister, Catherine elbowed through the jabbering crush of people. Then a small, familiar form darted across the confusion.

Alice was on the other side of the aisle, moving

toward her. She worked her way through the milling crowd and grabbed her mother's outstretched hand. "I wanted to go to communion, Mommy, but Father Tom wouldn't give me the Host . . ." she babbled.

"What are you doing here?" Catherine demanded.

"Get the fire department!" someone shouted up ahead.

Catherine pulled Alice toward the exit.

"Come on. We've got to get out of here."

As they followed the jostling flow of people, Catherine kept searching for Karen. They were almost at the lobby when she saw the smoke. Two men were pushing past the crowd. One held a fire extinguisher over his head, and the other was carrying blankets.

Alice shuffled behind, tugging at her mother's hand.

When Catherine glanced back she saw a piece of white lace trailing from Alice's raincoat pocket. It was Karen's veil.

Startled, Catherine snatched the veil from her daughter's pocket. "Where did you get this? Where's Karen? Where's your sister?" she cried.

Alice shrank back. "I found it on the floor. Maybe she dropped it. I was going to give it to her."

A loud shriek swiveled Catherine's head around.

"Get an ambulance!" someone shouted.

There was another shriek, and Catherine recognized her sister's hysterical wailing above the commotion.

"Let me go to her! I must go to her!" Annie was squalling.

Catherine pushed toward the sound of her sister's cries, dragging Alice behind her.

"Come on! Come with me!"

"No, Mommy. I don't want to!" Alice protested, trying to dig her heels into the floor.

But Catherine's desperate panic swept them both into the crowd of onlookers clogging the rear aisle.

Annie was being restrained by a fat man while Jim fluttered nearby, shielding their son Robert from the scuffle.

When Annie saw Catherine squeezing through the crowd, she broke away from the fat man and rushed to her.

"Catherine, go back! Don't go in!"

The despair in her sagging expression seared Catherine's awareness. A jolt of terror buckled her knees, and she stumbled into Annie's frantic arms.

"Where's Karen?" she yelled.

"Don't go back there!" Annie groaned, gripping her arms.

"Where's Karen?" Catherine pleaded, struggling to get free. "Where is she?"

"Stand back!" a man barked. "Let Father Tom through."

Silently the throng parted to allow Father Tom access to the smoky room.

Catherine strained against her sister's embrace, trying to follow. She stopped struggling when Tom emerged from the room and came toward them.

Annie released her sister's arms and crossed herself. "Oh, Catherine! She's dead. She's dead!"

Annie's wail slammed against Catherine's unbelieving brain as she looked at Father Tom.

"No, Tom. It's not true!" she whispered.

The brutal anguish twisting his face told her it was, and she collapsed in his arms, sobbing convulsively.

Alice stood a few feet away, watching them.

She saw her mother drop the veil and eased closer. Calmly, she picked up the veil, stuffed it in her pocket, and retreated to a vacant pew.

The only person who noticed was her aunt.

Blinking rapidly, as if suddenly awakened, Annie stared at the child who sat quietly, with her back to the crowd.

4

Forty-eight hours after receiving the news, Dominic Spages was on an eastbound jet, working on his second bourbon.

Ironic that it was Tom who called, he thought. Religion had been the largest factor in the breakup of his marriage.

His new wife Julia was sensual, uninhibited, and nondogmatic; all the traits Catherine rejected in favor of her rigid Catholicism. Their marriage and a successful career enabled him to enjoy the pleasures he could never share with Catherine—joys that washed away the frustration and guilt.

But the pain of Karen's death brought it all flooding back. She'd paid for his joys with her life. If he'd been there, perhaps she'd be alive today. If he hadn't been so selfish.

He wasn't even sure he'd be in time for the funeral, Dom mused, lifting his empty glass as the stewardess passed by. This time however, the delay wasn't due to selfishness. Julia was pregnant, and there'd been certain arrangements to be made at the office.

He'd failed Karen while she was alive, but not again. He planned to stay beyond the funeral until her murderer was found.

The first-class stewardess smiled hopefully at the handsome young businessman as she served a fresh bourbon, but she was disappointed. Dom had other things on his mind.

Until Karen's murder, he'd been guided by the belief that the divorce would ultimately help his children find fulfillment. He'd hoped his new life would provide an alternative to Catherine's narrow views. Instead, he had left them unprotected. As a father and as a man, it was time to pay the price for his beliefs. Just as Karen had paid.

He loved his daughters. It was only fierce devotion to the children that had kept him from leaving sooner. But it didn't matter now.

Dom drained his glass, trying to fill the emptiness. No matter how much he loved her, it wasn't enough, he reflected bitterly. His beautiful daughter was dead, and love didn't matter anymore.

The only way to atone for his failure was to find Karen's killer.

✠ ✠ ✠

It was sunny but extremely cold on the morning of Karen's funeral. The small group of mourners shivered, breath coming in frosty clouds as they watched the pallbearers carry the small white coffin to the open grave.

Parked a discreet distance from the funeral group, Captain Raymond Beame of the Paterson Homicide Squad drummed his fingers on the wheel of his unmarked car. Beame's bland, pudgy features effectively concealed his foul mood that morning.

One: he'd just had a fight with his wife, two: he didn't like psycho cases. And three: his assistant was becoming too damned ambitious. Spina was acting like some TV gumshoe on this thing.

Still, photographing the funeral made sense, Beame admitted ruefully. You never knew with these weirdos.

Behind him, Mike Spina adjusted the telescopic lens on his Pentax, methodically snapping pictures of everyone at the gravesite. He was younger than Beame, with dark, intelligent eyes and a brusque aggressive manner.

"The fat one didn't show up," he announced when he stopped to reload the camera. "That Alphonso."

Beame considered. What kind of degenerate would do something like that, he wondered unhappily. The bitch of it was, it could be anybody.

"Where was Alice?" he asked finally.

"The mother said she was helping the nuns."

"Did you talk to any of them?"

"Not yet."

"Find out exactly where she was."

Spina grunted unhappily, knowing it wouldn't be easy. Then he saw a taxi roll to a halt in front of the hearse. A tanned, well-built man in a black coat and tie paid the driver and walked to the gravesite.

"Who's that?" Spina murmured, hurriedly refocusing the camera.

Beame yawned. "That's the child's father. Dominic Spages. Save your film. I think we better look up this Alphonso character."

* * *

Annie resembled an outraged crow as she watched Dom approaching. Then her eyes darted to the people nearby.

"Well, at least he managed to get here before they put her in the ground," she declared loudly.

"Annie, please. Not now," Catherine gasped. She left Father Tom's side and hurried to embrace her ex-husband. "I'm so glad you're here," she whispered, straining to control her emotions.

Dom kissed her tenderly. "You can depend on me for anything you need."

He saw his daughter watching, and smiled. "Hello, Alice."

Alice's expression remained hostile as she moved closer to her mother.

At the conclusion of Father Tom's service, Annie briskly took charge of the transportation arrangements, assigning the mourners to the various limousines and cars making up the procession.

Her plump daughter Angela trailed behind uncertainly until Annie whirled on her. "Go!" she ordered, gesturing impatiently. "Go to your father. It's late."

As Angela ran to the limousine, Annie stalked toward her sister. Catherine was still beside the grave with Dom. They stood very close, talking quietly.

Annie broke in. "Sorry to rush you," she sniffed, "but mass begins at nine."

Dom nodded, his square-cut face impassive. "Thank you, Ann, we're ready," he said, taking Catherine's arm.

Annie marched ahead of them, infuriated by his polite indifference. When she saw Alice sitting alone in the rear of the limousine, her fury exploded.

"Make room for your mother and father," she blared, entering the car. "Sit on the fold-up."

Alice glowered. "I want to sit by my mother."

"You'll do as you're told."

"Please, Annie, there's plenty of room," Catherine said sharply. "And I want my daughter next to me."

Dom leaned on the door. "I can sit on the fold-up. No problem."

"Never mind—don't let *me* disturb you," Alice said icily, crawling out of the limousine. "I'll sit in the second car."

* * *

Annie's resentment was clearly evident as she aloofly served refreshments to the friends and relatives who crowded Catherine's apartment after the requiem mass.

Recognizing the suppressed rage on her pinched expression, her husband Jim kept well out of her way during the ceremonies. Robert and Angela wisely followed their father's example.

Cousin Fred and his wife were the last to leave.

"Please, don't hesitate to call," Fred repeated. "We want to do something. It's such a tragedy. Please don't hesitate to . . ."

"Thank you," Annie said crisply. "There's nothing more anyone can do. I'll be staying with my sister for as long as she needs me."

Both Catherine and Dom reacted to the statement. They looked at Annie, then each other. Alice flinched and stared down at her plate.

If Jim or the children were surprised, they knew better than to show it. Father and son sat quietly on the couch, biting their nails, while Angela hid behind a magazine.

Annie shut the door with a long, loud sigh of relief, then stalked to the table and began clearing off dishes.

Catherine touched her arm. "You don't have to stay. After all, you're only ten minutes away. Jim and the kids need you."

"Not another word," Annie insisted, patting her hand. "Jim wants me to stay. My Angela can take care of everything for him."

Dom leaned closer to Catherine. "I've made arrangements to stay in town a few days, so I'll be here if you need me."

She avoided his eyes. "Thanks Dom, but I'm sure you have to get back home."

"Look, Kay, maybe this is a bad time to bring it up, but . . . there's some things we have to talk about."

"The children!" Annie reminded vehemently.

Dom ignored her. "This is no ordinary situation. The . . ."

"Hush!" Annie insisted.

Dom slowly lifted his head.

"If you're concerned, ask them to leave. There's some things I want to know," he told Annie, his blue eyes cold.

Sensing the electric flare of hostility between them, Catherine stood up quickly.

"There's so much food left over," she mused, placing the unconsumed half of a cream cake in a box. "It's a shame to let it go to waste. Alice, take this box to Mr. Alphonso."

Expression blank, Alice obediently rose from her chair and took the box. "Okay, Mommy."

Annie squinted at her children. "Go with her. You can play in the back yard."

Cherub features veiling their contempt, Robert and Angela followed Alice to the door.

"Don't disappear—keep the noise down!" Annie warned, her shouts trailing after the trio as they skipped down the stairs.

They were still shouting in the apartment when the children reached the second landing.

Robert and Angela hung back, frightened but eager to see Alphonso the monster.

Alice's slightly bulging eyes regarded them smugly. Enjoying her moment of power, she turned and walked to the door with elaborate slowness.

The door opened as soon as she knocked.

The hairless, flab-layered heap of soiled, sweating humanity who presented himself drove Robert scampering down the stairs.

Angela held her ground, watching Alice.

"I heard everyone leave," Alphonso wheezed. "It's all over, huh?" He licked his lips and leered at Alice. "You die, they put you in the ground and it's over. Such a pretty girl, too. Such a shame, so little. Too pretty to wind up in a box."

Alice thrust the box of cake into his massive belly. "My mother thought you could use some cake. Fatty."

Alphonso's slitted eyes studied her closely as he took the box.

"God always takes the pretty ones," he spat maliciously. Then he smiled. "Thank your mother. Such a lovely lady."

"Wow!" Angela exclaimed after he shut the door. "His stomach is so big that if someone stuck him with a knife, he'd burst."

"He scares me," Robert whispered, coming closer.

Alice smiled at the closed door. "That ugly bastard doesn't scare me."

Robert giggled, excited by her boldness.

Angela glanced at the ceiling. "Come on, Alice," she urged. "Let's get out of here before my mother hears us."

Muffling their laughter, the trio hurried downstairs. At the bottom landing, Angela stopped and looked at her brother.

"Where are you going? We don't want *you* with us," she informed him loftily.

Confused, Robert watched them walk to the basement door, arms linked like conspirators. He lingered in the hall, wondering whether to return to his parents until he remembered he'd have to pass Alphonso's door.

The memory drove him outside, into the sunlight.

* * *

Dom pounded on the table, face knotted with disbelief. "Goddammit, Annie. The child was murdered. Don't you understand what that means? It takes a screwed-up person to do a job like that. Aren't you afraid? He could come after Alice or Angela. What's the matter with you people? Aren't you listening to me?"

Annie clutched her throat. "You don't know what we've been through. You barely made it to the funeral."

"Annie—please—don't start," Catherine snapped.

Triumphantly, Annie leaned across the table. "You have no idea of what *I'm* talking about. Do you?" She smirked, voice heavy with implication.

Dom glanced at Catherine. "What's she trying to say?"

She gestured helplessly and turned away.

Suddenly aware of an odd tension between the two sisters, Dom swung around and glared at Jim. "What's this all about?"

Startled by the sudden attention, Jim cringed against the sofa, watery eyes blinking from his wife's frown to Dom's clenched fists.

"Alice was the last one in the church," he blurted abruptly. Immediately regretting his folly, Jim struggled to his feet and scurried to his wife's side.

Dom shrugged. "So? What's that supposed to mean?"

Catherine slapped the table. "Stop it! I won't listen to this again."

The intensity of her outburst splashed across Dom's confusion like ice water. "Are you trying to imply that Alice had something to do with the murder?" he asked, eyes fixed on Annie.

Her expression wavered and she grasped Jim's arm defensively. "I'm not saying anything of the kind. My God, don't I love that child? She's like one of my own," Annie chanted as if reciting a prayer. Then the vengeful grimace returned. "I practically raised her," she reminded acidly.

"I know all about that, Annie," Dom sighed.

"You don't know all about anything. All you know is to send a check once a month."

Catherine cut in, voice edged with hysteria. "Please, Annie, not now."

Her sister clutched her breast as if mortally wounded. "It would never occur to you that I'm trying to protect her, would it?"

"Protect her from what?" Dom snorted.

Catherine sprang from her chair like a white-faced tigress, fierce menace burning through her tears. "Are you so sure you're trying to protect her?"

Her question flooded the room with embarrassed silence. For the sake of her precious, lost daughter, Catherine held back her rage. "If you don't mind," she said curtly, "I'm going to lie down."

The moment she closed the bedroom door, Annie broke the quiet.

"You saw the photographers at the church," she hissed.

When Dom didn't react, Jim hastily nodded agreement. "Yes, that's right."

"The police *do* investigate a murder, you know," she reminded, squinting at Dom.

"I still don't understand what this has to do with Alice."

Annie leaned closer. "Everyone knew she was the last one in the church. They want to talk to her. They think she may have seen someone."

Her voice lowered. "What if the police find out about the veil?"

Dom blinked. "What about the veil?"

"She had Karen's veil in her pocket."

It took a second before the full meaning of Annie's smug whisper sliced across his understanding like an icy razor. "Jesus Christ, she probably picked up the veil from the floor!" he exploded hoarsely.

Dom lurched from his chair, bunched muscles in his jaw and neck flushing red as he strained to control his emotions. "Did you bother to ask *her* where she got it from?"

Annie and Jim exchanged a nervous glance.

Dom bottled up his anger. This wasn't the time, he told himself. Catherine needed him now. He turned away from their accusing silence and stalked out of the dining room.

Annie's shrewd gaze followed him all the way to the bedroom, eyes glittering with disapproval, and odd anticipation.

There was nothing left but disapproval when they returned to her husband. Annie shot Jim a withering, knowing expression, then began clearing the dishes away.

Jim rose quickly to help, still wishing he'd kept his mouth shut about the veil.

5

The Paterson Homicide Division was headquartered in a bleak nineteenth-century building behind City Hall.

Two uniformed officers were stationed behind a high, paneled bar at the end of a large, dimly lit reception hall. The bar was distinguished by an oversized brass foot rail of the kind commonly seen in old saloons. The police officers' elevated position endowed them with an aura of regal aloofness, which usually heightened the insecurity of those compelled to do business there.

Dominic Spages was the exception. He approached the bar with the easy confidence of a man at home with authority. His voice carried the same quality when he addressed the duty officer.

"I have an appointment with Detective Captain Beame."

Quickly appraising the expensive coat and direct tone, the duty officer nodded politely.

"Take the elevator over there to the second floor. Go to your right. You'll pass some lockers, and you'll see the room. There's a sign on the door."

The elevator was a rattling cage better suited for hauling freight than visitors. As the doors opened the wizened policewoman inside looked up from her clipboard. Her leathery face lit up when she saw the police officer who entered behind Dom.

"How's it goin', Joe?"

"Okay, Mary," he returned genially.

"Floor?" she inquired, finger poised over the buttons.

"Two, please," Dom said.

But when the elevator rumbled into motion, it began to descend. "Oops!" Mary laughed. "Hey, I just came from the basement."

The elevator stopped at the floor below, and the doors slid open on a gray concrete storeroom. Two janitors were leaning against the exposed plumbing, deeply engrossed in their discussion.

"Why the hell are they having an auction for four bikes?" one man demanded as they stepped into the elevator. "Hi, Mary."

He looked back at his companion. "Before they auction those bikes, I'm gonna steal the red one."

Mary and her policeman friend began to laugh. "No, you don't—I've got my bid for that one," she declared, shaking her finger.

As the elevator rose again, the other janitor broke the chuckling silence.

"Hey, Mary, what's the scoop on that Spages case?"

The detached amusement faded from Dom's face as he watched the wiry little policewoman.

Her smile was gone as well. "They know as

much about that as they know about those bikes," she said grimly. "I can tell you this much: I sat in on the line-up yesterday. There is no encouragement there."

She shrugged her shoulders and snorted. "I could have told them that pulling in the regulars was a waste of time. If you want my opinion . . ."

It was interrupted by the opening of the doors. Dom waited intently for her to continue as the doors closed again.

Mary jabbed the hold button and looked up.

"Hey, didn't you want the second floor? This is it."

Dom left the elevator reluctantly, one statement she'd made tumbling through his thoughts. "They know as much about that as they know about those bikes." Although seemingly hopeless, it somehow reassured his decision to begin his own investigation of Karen's murder.

When Dom found the office, Detective Raymond Beame was glumly investigating the interior of a sandwich.

Dom hesitated at the door. "Captain Beame?"

"That's me, come in," Beame drawled, still preoccupied with his sandwich. He took a plastic spoon from a paper cup nearby and carefully scraped mayonnaise from the bread. As if just aware of Dom's presence, he smiled and held up his spoon.

"I've been telling her for twenty-two years—not too much mayonnaise," he explained ruefully. "Please sit down."

Dom unbuttoned his coat, looking around the cramped, overcrowded room for an available chair. Both desks were piled with papers, as were the chairs, bookcases, and stacks of boxes between. *This is the office of the man who's supposed to find my daughter's killer,* Dom thought as he cleared some newspapers and manila envelopes from a chair and pulled it beside Beame's desk.

The detective contentedly munched his sandwich until he noticed Dom's expression. He stopped chewing and met the cold, steady stare.

"Sorry about your daughter."

Recognizing his sincerity, Dom nodded. But there was little else about the pudgy shirt-sleeved detective that comforted him.

"How about some coffee?" Beame suggested genially. "Or maybe—" he lifted the dripping bag from his cup—"some hot tea."

Dom shook his head.

Undaunted, Beame plucked a wrapped object from the litter on his desk. "How about a sandwich? She always makes two, but I never eat the second."

"No, thank you," Dom said stiffly.

Beame wiped his mouth with a paper napkin. "You must have a lot of questions."

"You're goddamned right I do. I was hoping you'd have some leads."

"We're checking a few things." Beame leaned back and took a bite of his sandwich. "As a matter of fact, someone is in your neighborhood right now, doing legwork."

Unimpressed, Dom watched him reach into a drawer and extract a salt shaker. "Are you doing anything to protect Catherine . . . and my daughter?"

The shaker paused above Beame's sandwich. "What makes you think they'll be another attack on your family?" he asked, eyes alert.

Dom's face remained impassive. "I don't know. I couldn't imagine anyone killing Karen."

Beame salted his meat. "Most murders are committed by someone who knew the victim," he observed thoughtfully.

"If it's someone who knew Karen, why did he

pick the church?" Dom countered. "It seems pretty stupid to take a chance in front of all those people."

"Yes. I've been thinking that myself"—Beame speculated, chair squeaking as he leaned back—"in the middle of a crowded church he drags the body across a crowded floor and carefully places it in a chest." His gaze drifted to the portrait of John F. Kennedy on the wall. "Very deliberate, wouldn't you say?"

Dom shrugged. "Why in God's name did he try to set fire to my daughter?"

Beame shook his head. "He didn't try to set fire to the church." He popped the last of his sandwich into his mouth. "Do you mind if I talk to Alice today?" he asked casually.

Dom tensed. "Where's that going to get you?"

"Alice was the last one to come into the church. She may have seen something," Beame droned patiently. "A detail that means nothing to her may set us in the right direction, for example. Like where exactly she found the veil."

Making an effort to conceal his rising agitation, Dom considered the request. There was something in the detective's bland tone he didn't like at all. Something insidious.

Beame was still waiting for his answer when Detective Mike Spina entered.

Noting his partner's brash grin, Beame quickly spoke up before Spina could upset things with a careless remark. "Mike Spina, this is Dominic Spages," he drawled heartily. "I've just been asking his permission to talk to Alice."

To Beame's relief, Spina caught the hint. He diluted his grin to a disarming smile, as he slowly unbuttoned his coat.

"I was just down in your neighborhood. Sorry about your trouble."

When Dom didn't respond, Spina walked to

the coffeepot beside his desk. "Boy, it's raw out there. Jesus Christ, Ray, the car defroster still isn't working."

Beame didn't answer, wishing Spina would find something to keep him quiet. He was disappointed when Spina held up the coffeepot.

"Would you like a cup, Mr. Spages?" he fawned, overworking the smile.

"No, thanks." Dom kept his eyes on Beame. "About that veil," he said firmly. "It's obvious to me that Alice came in just *after* the murder."

Beame folded his arms, expression dubious.

"I spoke to her, and she said it was on the floor when she came in," Dom explained. "Karen must have dropped it in the struggle."

Unfortunately, Spina couldn't stay out of it. "Mr. Spages, how did Alice know it was Karen's veil?" he snapped. "I checked. They're all exactly alike." He grinned triumphantly at Beame. "They're all purchased from the same store."

Sighing, Beame examined his fingernails. If there'd been any hope, it was gone. Spina's smart-assed deductions would only make Spages hostile.

He was right.

"Alice never said it was Karen's veil," Dom declared angrily. "Everyone just assumed it was."

Spina swaggered closer. "According to your sister-in-law, Alice said it was Karen's veil."

"You don't know Annie. She's always jumping to conclusions—especially when it comes to Alice."

"But your wife didn't disagree with her," Spina taunted, chin thrust forward aggressively.

"My wife has been under a lot of strain."

Although secretly pleased by Dom's refusal to knuckle under, Beame was curious about something.

"Does your sister-in-law *dislike* your daughter?" he asked.

"Yes," Dom said calmly. "But I think it's more accurate to say she doesn't like me."

Spina pounced, again too soon. "Do you really think your sister-in-law dislikes you that much? Enough that she'd want to implicate your daughter in a murder?"

The impact of his last statement cracked Dom's patience. "I don't like the way you're questioning me," he growled. "You really must be desperate to start on a twelve-year-old girl."

Regretfully, Beame watched him jump to his feet. As Dom turned, the detective knew what he'd say.

"On second thought, I don't think it's a good idea for you to talk to Alice. She's been through enough hell."

He was almost at the door when he stopped and looked back. "I came down here to see if there was anything I could do to help," he mused, his voice choked with disgust.

Beame accepted his contempt with a weary smile. "Do you really think I'm looking to pin a murder on a little girl?"

Seeing Dom's hesitation, he made a last try. "I need to talk to Alice. Can you help me with that?"

Through his outrage and disappointment, Dom recognized the detective's basic honesty. He wavered, exploring the request until he saw the expectant gleam in Spina's eyes. *That rat bastard would suck his mother's blood for a promotion,* Dom decided, hostility sealing off all doubts.

"I think it would be best if I prepared Catherine first. I'll call you later," he said.

"Would you be able to get back to us by—say —three o'clock?" Beame persisted.

Dom nodded, anxious to leave.

When they were alone, Beame regarded Spina with undisguised disdain. "Well, you sure fixed that one. Had him ready to sign until you butt in with that veil stuff. Sella's has been supplying St. Michael's with veils ever since I can remember."

Spina moved quickly to his coat, pulled a manila envelope from the inside pocket, and tossed it on Beame's desk.

"With this report from St. Michael's school, maybe we won't need his signature."

* * *

The phone in the rectory rang just as Mrs. Tredoni set a steaming bowl of vegetable soup before Father Tom. He automatically moved to answer, but Mrs. Tredoni restrained him with a firm hand.

"It's time to eat. No calls," she reminded. "I'll take it."

Her narrow bony face was taut with indignation as she bustled to answer the persistent ringing. They never gave Father Tom any rest, she thought. Always calling him for the least thing. They didn't care about his health.

"St. Michael's Rectory," she barked into the phone.

"Father Tom, please. This is Dominic Spages."

"I'm sorry. Father does not like to be disturbed at mealtimes," Mrs. Tredoni said crisply. "If you give me your number, I can have him call you."

"Just tell him it's Dom Spages."

"I don't care who it is. Those are the rules."

"This is urgent. Please call him."

"Don't raise your voice to me," Mrs. Tredoni shouted. "If I gave in every time somebody told me that, he'd never eat a meal without interruption."

As her noisy protests filtered into the next room, Father Tom left the table and went to the wall extension in the hall. Experience had taught him that Mrs. Tredoni could be overly protective.

Tom carefully lifted the phone, covering the mouthpiece until he recognized Dom's voice. "It's okay, Mrs. Tredoni," he said.

With a sharp grunt of disapproval she hung up.

"Sorry," Tom apologized. "She's doing it for my own good. I gave her specific instructions to put you through, but . . ."

"Listen, I'm down here at the police station," Dom interrupted. "Do you know what those bastards are trying to do to Alice?"

"Did they mention anything about the school?"

"No. What about the school?"

"Well, they came by and took Alice's records," Tom said, trying to make the affair sound routine. The stunned pause told him he hadn't succeeded.

"I don't believe those sons of bitches," Dom muttered.

"Take it easy. I know Beame. He's not that kind of guy."

"Yeah? Well, the bastard wants to question Alice. He wants my permission."

Tom eased off the sensitive topic. "Have you called Catherine?"

"Yes. I told her we were coming over."

"All right. Hold on then. I'll meet you at police headquarters. I want to talk to you alone before we see her. I've got something important to discuss. I'm leaving now," he added, cutting off Dom's questions.

After replacing the phone, Tom moved briskly to the front hall. "I'll be gone for a couple of hours, Mrs. Tredoni!" he called, pulling his coat from the closet.

"Will you be home for dinner?" she shouted back.

Receiving no answer, she hurried out of the

kitchen, but by the time she reached the front hall, it was empty. The open closet offered mute testimony that he'd left the house.

"I know his couple of hours," Mrs. Tredoni grumbled as she shuffled to the dining room. "That phone call. I knew it was going to happen."

She heaved a deep, despairing sigh when she saw the unfinished bowl of soup. "That's precisely why I hate to interrupt his meals," she fretted. "There is a good reason for every rule."

Her own life had taught her the value of discipline, she reflected as she cleared off the dishes. Left homeless by the war, she'd come to America with nothing. But she'd studied hard with the nuns and soon could speak well enough to be given a job at the rectory as a scullery maid. A year later, she was chief housekeeper and social secretary.

She'd held her position through the regimes of three pastors, and her rules had always been strictly enforced—until Father Tom was made head of St. Michael's.

Mrs. Tredoni's haggard features softened into a beatific smile of forgiveness as she entered the kitchen. It wasn't his fault, she knew. None of the others had ever done so much for the parish. Father Tom was totally devoted to his flock—not like the old one upstairs.

Her scowl returned, and she glanced at the ceiling. During the last years of the monsignor's reign, nobody wanted his counsel or his company; and the rectory was usually empty. The old prelate ran the parish like a tyrant until the stroke confined him to a room on the second floor.

It was a blessing when Father Tom took over. The rectory became alive again—alive with Christ's sanctifying grace. There was a constant flow of calls, meetings, visits, and joyous enthusiasm.

"Maybe too much enthusiasm," Mrs. Tredoni brooded. That's why the rules were always being ignored. Father Tom was a holy saint, but everyone wanted to take advantage of his goodness.

All these people were pulling him apart. That's why the rules were there—to protect him.

And that's why she was there, Mrs. Tredoni mused, filling the sink with soapy water. To protect him.

✠ ✠ ✠

Catherine felt like an intruder in her daughter's bedroom.

She fumbled through the clothes in Karen's bureau with a furtive sense of shame, as if she were looting a tomb. But her need overpowered any scruples she had left. Lovingly she pressed a worn sweater to her face. It smelled of Karen.

The familiar odor filled the emptiness in her soul as she knelt in the darkness.

"Alice, put that knife down!"

Her sister's sharp voice pierced the comforting silence. Empty again, Catherine prayed for the noise to stop. Didn't they understand that Karen was dead? This constant bickering was obscene. If it didn't stop, she'd break down completely.

"That's too heavy! Be careful!"

The shout was punctuated by a crash—instantly followed by a shrill jabber.

"What did I tell you?"

"Don't hit me! I didn't mean it!"

When Catherine rushed into the kitchen, she saw Annie shaking Alice by the shoulders. The child flailed wildly, trying to strike back. "Don't hit me! Don't hit me!"

"What's the matter?" Catherine cried. "What happened?" Then she saw the large white sunburst of spilled milk and shattered glass on the floor. "Oh my God! What a mess!"

Annie continued to hold Alice at bay.

"I'm not going to hit you!" she yelled. "Have I ever hit you? That's the trouble. You need a few good smacks."

Alice pulled free. "You liar. You were, too!"

"Alice, don't move!" Catherine warned. "You're walking on glass!"

Ignoring her, Annie advanced toward Alice. "She called me a liar. By God, now I *am* going to hit you!"

"Annie!"

The desperation in Catherine's voice stopped her sister short.

"You see, she *was* going to hit me," Alice pleaded, retreating to her mother's side. "It was just an accident."

Catherine recognized the frenzied appeal in her daughter's eyes, but was helpless to answer. "Be still—you'll cut yourself," she said weakly.

"You see this mess? And I just finished cleaning. Didn't I tell her to be careful? She never listens to me."

The rasping complaint sparked Catherine's resistance, and she cut Annie off. "Alice said it was an accident." She smiled at her daughter. "Tell Aunt Annie you're sorry."

Mouth locked, Alice turned her back.

Annie nodded in grim satisfaction.

"It's always an accident with her. But accidents don't happen when you use the stick. You give in, Kay—that's what's wrong."

Alice whirled, stubby features taut with fury. "You hate me. I didn't do it on purpose," she insisted, stamping toward the table.

"Stand still," Catherine ordered. "I want you to shut up and be careful of that broken glass."

As Alice stopped, her heel came down on a glass fragment with a slow, deliberate crunch.

"Now she's tracking it all over the place," Annie shouted.

"Go over to the table and stay put while we clean this mess up."

Responding instantly to her mother's soft command, Alice walked to the kitchen table.

"I told her it was too heavy, and she goes right ahead and does it anyway," Annie muttered, vigorously mopping the floor. "What kind of idiot carries a gallon of milk and a sandwich at the same time?"

As if expecting an answer, she glanced at Catherine. "This," she stated, lifting her mop as evidence, "is why she should be back in school."

Alice jumped from her chair, eyes bulging. "I'm not going back to school. I'm never going back." She rushed to her mother. "I want to stay with you."

Catherine held her close, searching for some last dreg of strength she could give to Alice.

"Your mother doesn't need you," Annie said vengefully. "*I'm* here. You belong in school."

"She does, too!" Alice wailed. "I'm not going! I won't go!"

Catherine lashed out angrily. "Why must you keep insisting about this school business?"

"With the trouble she's been having, she can't afford to miss a single day."

Catherine felt Alice stiffen and held her tighter. "I spoke to Father Tom, and we agreed that Monday is soon enough."

"Not Monday, Mommy, please!" Alice moaned.

Annie clasped her hands in resignation. "Have it your way, Catherine. But remember what they say. The devil makes work for idle hands." Lips pursed, she peered ominously at Alice. "The child belongs in school. My Angela's heard plenty about this one."

Alice twisted loose and lurched toward her aunt. "This is my house!" she shrieked. Then she stopped, limbs trembling and face contorted with malice. "I can't wait till you leave," she declared fervently.

Catherine gripped her arm. "I forbid you to talk that way to your aunt."

The touch of her mother's hand seemed to calm Alice. Except for a nervous twitch below one eye, her face was placid and her tone submissive. "Mommy, I'm sorry I dropped it. She makes me so nervous, I do everything wrong."

"You don't mean what you're saying," Catherine said softly, stroking her hair. "Aunt Annie loves you. She does things only for your own good." Smiling, she lifted Alice's chin. "Now, admit it. If you'd just listened to her, you wouldn't have dropped the milk."

Alice pulled away. "Why is she always right? You always take her side."

"That's enough," Catherine said. "Come with me."

Alice took her mother's hand and quietly followed her to the sink. Catherine took a towel from the rack, knelt down, and began wiping the milk stains from her daughter's shoes.

"Mommy does need you, dear," she whispered. "But you must realize that Aunt Annie is very generous to come live with us."

"Yeah, sure," Alice sighed.

"And I don't want to hear any more about not going back to school. You must go back." Catherine looked at her tenderly. "We both have to get back to our usual lives," she said, her voice husky with emotion. "I know how much you miss Karen. So do I."

She bent her head quickly so Alice wouldn't see the tears.

Alice lowered a tentative hand. "I'll be your . . ."

Catherine stood up, accidentally brushing the hand away.

"Sorry, darling." She reached out to smooth her daughter's hair. When Alice stepped back, her mother perceived how deeply she'd been offended by the foolish incident.

The child's extremely sensitive, Catherine realized. *I'm so distraught, I've forgotten her feelings.* She was like an open wound. She also understood that Alice felt unwanted these days. She needed a sense of belonging.

Catherine smiled brightly, bending closer to her. "You're my big girl, right?"

"I guess so," Alice mumbled, trying to return the smile.

"Then you can help me." Catherine moved to the counter where she kept the household bills, picked up a check, and held it out to Alice.

She eyed the check suspiciously. "What can I do?"

"You can take the rent check down to Mr. Alphonso."

Alice shrugged and took the check.

"Now, that will really help me . . . and Aunt Annie," Catherine beamed. "Play in the yard for a while, and as soon as this mess is cleaned up, we'll call you. And you know what?"

"What?" Alice asked, face illuminated by expectation.

"I'll make you a new snack," Catherine promised. "I'll make your favorite—peanut butter and jelly."

A shadow fell across Alice's expression. "That's okay but . . . that's Karen's favorite."

Although stricken by guilt, Catherine tried to keep her voice light. "Oh, that's right. I'm sorry, darling. I meant grilled cheese. With a tomato on it. Just the way you like it."

Alice nodded impassively.

"Okay, thanks. But I . . ." She looked across the room at her aunt and hesitated.

"But what, darling?" Catherine prompted, moving closer. "Tell me."

"I thought you were talking about my radio. Remember? You promised."

Catherine smiled. "I remember. And tomorrow we'll both go shopping, okay?"

Alice's expression brightened and she gave Catherine a loud kiss. "Okay, Mommy. Thanks."

Relieved by her daughter's oversight of the careless error, Catherine watched Alice walk to the hall and pull her yellow slicker from the hook behind the door. From now on, she resolved, there'd be no more mistakes like that. She couldn't expect Alice to replace her sister.

"We're never going to agree on how to handle that child, but your methods don't seem to work very well," Annie droned.

"She's going through a lot," Catherine reminded curtly. "My God, this is a bad time. She really loved her sister."

Expression stony and remote, Annie turned her attention to the wet glass littering the floor.

Wordlessly, Catherine moved to help her. Some minutes later, as they cleared away the last vestiges of the accident, Annie paused.

"Did you find the crucifix?"

Annoyed by the question, Catherine continued sweeping bits of glass into the dustpan.

"No. I went through all her clothes. I'm sure it was lost at the church, but I allowed myself to hope a little. Don't worry—when Vinnie gets around to sweeping, he'll find it."

"Well, it's not in Alice's drawers."

The blunt statement jolted Catherine upright.

"Why did you do that? I told you I would ask her. Why don't you trust her?" she demanded fiercely.

Annie backed toward the sink, eyes blinking indignantly. "I know how important that cross is to you," she whined defensively. "I never can do anything right anymore." She straightened her shoulders, face pinched with self-pity. "Maybe I should leave, like Alice said."

Catherine weighed her appeal coldly. Alice was a problem, but Annie was another. It was like having a spy in the house. She'd searched the child's things as if she were a criminal. Certainly her sister was upsetting Alice with that kind of attitude.

"You know I want you here," she said gently. "And Alice does, too. But . . . maybe it *would* be better if we were alone for a while. . . ."

✠ ✠ ✠

Alice could hear them arguing as she walked down the stairs. She knew her aunt hated her, but she didn't care. Soon she'd be in her sanctuary, where nobody could hurt her. The *new* sanctuary.

The old sanctuary wasn't secret enough and was too far away. This one was perfect. Aunt Annie could search through her room all she wanted, Alice gloated. No one could find the secret treasures in her sanctuary. Not even Karen could.

But before she could go there, she had something to do.

Moving as quietly as possible, she approached Alphonso's door, and stood listening to the scratchy opera music wafting into the hall.

Inside, his shapeless bulk wedged into a sagging armchair, Alphonso contemplated the grandeur of Verdi.

Eyes closed, he stroked the kitten curled at his neck, blissfully immersed in the music until a creaking sound pulled his attention to the door.

It was closed. Nothing moved except the cats prowling silently through the littered room. Alphonso sighed and drifted back to the opera.

A second creak lifted his eyelids open. "Come in, Alice," he called in a bored tone.

Receiving no answer, Alphonso raised his voice. "You heard me. What's the matter? Are you afraid?"

When Alice peered around the door, Alphonso was sitting in front of the phonograph with his eyes closed. "You can come in," he droned without looking up. "I won't hurt you."

Warily, Alice entered the apartment. Satisfied that Alphonso was intent on his music, she took a few steps closer.

"How did you know it was me?"

Alphonso's eyes rolled open. "I know everything about little Alice," he confided mysteriously. He pressed a grimy finger to his lips. "Shh . . . listen." His finger left his mouth and began moving in time to the music.

Alice ignored the suggestion. "I have the rent check. I was going to slide it under the door."

The kitten perched on Alphonso's mountainous belly playfully pawed at the finger as it continued conducting the orchestra.

Impatience prodded Alice's temper. She couldn't stay in this crummy toilet. She had to get to the sanctuary before her aunt called her.

Her face screwed up with loathing, she looked around the rubbish-cluttered room for a place to deposit the check. "Where do you want me to put this? There's so much junk around the place, I bet you never clean it." Her lips curled back in a challenging sneer. "It smells of cat pee."

Alphonso's finger stopped in midair. "Didn't your mother tell you to give me the check?" he asked haughtily.

"What's the matter, Fatty? Stuck in your chair?"

Alphonso turned, his mouth almost hidden behind the flab bulging from his neck. His beady eyes were blank, but his accusing whine betrayed his annoyance.

"What did you break?" he taunted. "Clumsy Alice."

Seeing her flinch, he baited her a bit more. "You don't like your aunt, do you?"

"I don't like you."

"You know why you don't like us?" he asked, his gaze bright with malice. "It's because your aunt and I are two very perceptive people. We know what you did at the church. I can't wait to tell your father about you."

To prevent her from answering, he turned up the volume on the phonograph, leaned back, and closed his eyes.

The thundering blare crashed against Alice's numbed expression as she stared at him.

"What have you got to tell?" she shouted above the music.

Alphonso continued stroking his kitten.

Trembling with rage, Alice crushed the rent check into a ball and hurled it at him.

"Who's gonna believe you anyway? What do you know?" she jeered, turning to leave.

Suddenly the music stopped. Alphonso heaved himself erect and waddled toward her, kitten clutched against his quivering breasts like a baby.

"I know what you have downstairs."

The barbed statement pulled her back from the door. "Have you been snooping through my things?" Alice snarled.

His tongue flicked over his slack lips, hooded eyes impassive, like a gray toad regarding a scorpion. "Your things?"

His eyes widened in mock surprise. "They're not yours." He began stroking the kitten. "The dead have ways," Alphonso crooned maliciously. "The dead don't rest easy."

Transfixed by fear, Alice watched him move closer. She didn't understand what he intended to do until it was too late. As she dove for the door, he grabbed her arm and swung her viciously, slamming her against the wall. A moment later, his putrid flesh smothered her struggles.

She squirmed helplessly, cries muffled by the crushing pressure of Alphonso's belly.

"You better let me out or I'll scream. And my mother will call the police."

"The police were already here," he announced ominously. Then he pressed harder and began rocking back and forth. "And if they come back, I'm going . . . to take them . . . downstairs. . . ."

Through her desperate revulsion, Alice could hear the monotonous thud of the still-revolving record. It seemed to be keeping time to Alphonso's hoarse wheezing as he rubbed against her.

"Let me go, you weirdo!" she screamed, flailing blindly at the foul smelling blob engulfing her.

"Go ahead . . . and cry out . . ." he gasped. "Go ahead . . . thief!" His voice became a shuddering moan and he rocked faster, flesh rolling convulsively over her struggling body.

Alice twisted one hand free, and with the deadly reflex of a karate expert, raked Alphonso's chest until her clawed fingers found the kitten. She pulled the kitten off his body and squeezed its neck.

"Get away from me, you bastard," she hissed, squeezing tight. "Get away or I'll kill your cat."

Alphonso stumbled back, blubbering frantically. "Don't hurt kitty. Oh, don't hurt my princess."

Alice edged toward the door, dangling the kitten between them. "You pushed up against me once before, you disgusting slob. You'll never do that again."

The kitten's tiny red tongue protruded from its gaping mouth as Alice squeezed harder.

"Oh, no!" Alphonso squealed. "Please!"

With a triumphant smirk, Alice dropped the kitten and walked calmly into the hall.

Alphonso fell to his knees as the terrified animal streaked under the bed. "Oh, my poor beauty. Come to Daddy. That bitch! I'd like to kill her!"

* * *

Alice was impervious to the curses trailing her down the stairs. She could handle that fat bastard. She could even have him arrested for what he did, she reflected. But even that pleasant possibility didn't ease her depression.

The filthy weirdo had somehow found her sanctuary. It wasn't secret anymore—the holy secret that made it invulnerable.

Her only defense against Aunt Annie was destroyed.

And Karen.

Her sister could find her now that the holy seal of invisibility had been broken.

She felt somewhat better when she opened the door in the entrance hall and slipped into the familiar darkness of the basement stairway.

The dim light leaking through a slatted window enabled her to make out the squat outline of the furnace as she crossed the basement floor. There was an unused coal bin next to the oil furnace that was crammed with old furniture, broken tools, and stored junk.

Alice slowly edged through the maze until she reached a massive bookcase. She eased through a narrow space between the bookcase and some stacked crates, then took a book of matches from her pocket and struck a light.

She was standing in a small space, walled off by the bookcase and crates. There was just enough room for a rickety bureau and a chair. As Alice inspected her sanctuary, the match went out.

She lit another and walked inside. There was a candle in a jar on top of the bureau.

When Alice lit the candle, its expanding glow illuminated the porcelain face of a doll that was propped up beside it. It was Karen's doll.

Its eyes were closed in serene slumber as Alice moved to the other treasures of her sanctuary. The photograph of her standing with her father at the zoo. Her white prayerbook. The icepick. The jar of cockroaches with air holes punched into the lid.

Everything was there in its place.

Suddenly afraid, she knelt down and pulled a suitcase from its hiding place beneath the bureau. She opened it carefully, heart pounding as she checked its contents.

Nothing seemed disturbed.

The white veil on the folded white dress, and beneath it, the smiling lady mask. Alice lifted the pink plastic mask to her face.

Everything was exactly as she'd left it, Alice speculated, but she couldn't be sure. She shut the suitcase and shoved it beneath the bureau. The fat bastard. How did he find out about her secret place? She'd have to find another sanctuary. Somewhere completely secret and holy. Where she'd be completely safe.

Mask still covering her face, Alice rose and examined the roaches imprisoned in the jar. Their hairlike antennae twitched, as if in greeting.

She wondered if she should punch more holes in the lid with the icepick, then decided against it. Her eyes moved to the white prayerbook. It was the book for her First Communion—the one she never got to use.

Then she looked at the photograph of her father. It was the last time he'd taken her out alone.

Alice put the mask aside and took a crumpled napkin from her pocket with a festive flourish. She carefully unwrapped a crumb of cheese and placed it beside the jar. Then she tapped the jar's lid vigorously, driving the roaches to the bottom. She twisted the lid until it was almost open before picking up the cheese. She gave the lid a final twist, lifted quickly, thrust the cheese inside, and slammed the cover shut.

Everyone hates me, but I know a way to fix them. Aunt Annie, Alphonso, the whole rotten bunch, Alice gloated, screwing the lid tight. *They'll all be sorry they tried to hurt me.*

As Alice watched the roaches crawl over the cheese, the beautiful plastic lady smiled up at her.

6

It was raining hard when Father Tom picked Dom up at police headquarters.

They drove aimlessly for a while, the steady tick of the windshield wiper filling the long gaps in their conversation.

Dom was cordial enough, responding readily to Father Tom's reminiscences of old friends and good times. But he retained a certain distance. Father Tom took his time, trying to draw out the reason for Dom's cool reserve and hoping to re-establish their once-familiar closeness.

"I guess I'll always feel a little guilty," Dom mused, as if in answer to Father Tom's thoughts.

"What for?"

"It seems I've forced you into the role of father to my kids. I should be . . ."

Father Tom cut him off. "Nobody forced me into anything. You of all people should know better than that. I'm involved because I want to be."

Dom shook his head angrily. "You know, when you first called, I didn't want to come."

Father Tom didn't answer.

"I can't help it. I feel I don't belong here anymore."

"That's understandable."

"Julia understood it, too," Dom said ruefully. "But she felt strongly I should come. I guess that's what pushed my decision. Even though she's pregnant she feels . . ." He scowled, rummaging for words to express his emotion.

Father Tom kept his eyes on the rain-misted streets.

"I guess she knows that part of me will always be back here with Catherine and the kids," Dom blurted. "I mean . . . Alice is my . . ."

"Julia was right," Tom said softly. "You have a responsibility here. How is she, by the way?"

"Fine."

The subject of Dom's second wife stirred deep private concerns, but Father Tom kept his tone cheerful. "When is the baby due?"

But Dom wasn't listening. "It's a goddamn shame!" he exploded. "She should have a husband to share this grief with. She deserves something!"

Knowing there was nothing he could say, Father Tom stared ahead as the monotonous ticking of the wipers measured the silence.

When Dom spoke again, his voice was calm and pensive. "It's strange how things work out."

"How so?"

"I remember when we were in high school. You were the one always goofing off. I spent half my time getting you out of trouble. Now the roles seem to be reversed."

He grinned at Father Tom. "Remember the prom? I'm dancing close to Catherine, and you yell over the mike, 'Hey, Dom, leave six inches for the Holy Ghost.' "

Both men began laughing. Their exuberant glee seemed to recharge the drained link between them, and they kept on for long minutes, unwilling to let the connection fade.

As their chuckles dissolved into the impassive beat of the wiper, Dom looked away. "Still, I don't see why you didn't tell Catherine. If things were that bad at school, she should have been the first to know."

Regret choked off Father Tom's elation. "It wasn't that serious until recently."

Dom felt his suspicions return. Although his friendship with the priest went back to the days when he, Catherine, and Tom were the Three Musketeers of St. Michael's High, that didn't mean he knew the Father Tom sitting beside him today.

He was glad he hadn't revealed his true reason for coming. He'd intended to help find Karen's murderer, but now he saw there were other matters to solve first. *Why were they hounding the poor kid?* Dom wondered. *Because she was neurotic? Because she was rebellious?* It seemed incredible but they were trying to railroad Alice —the police, Annie, and even Father Tom.

"If it wasn't serious then, why is it suddenly serious now?" he asked, voice taut. "I mean, you've been telling me about deliberate vandalism and assault."

The priest paused, his youthful face lined with self-doubt and sorrow. "They weren't sure," he explained carefully. "They couldn't be sure Alice actually did anything on purpose. She has a knack for making things look like accidents." He glanced at Dom.

"I thought I could handle things quietly. She

used to talk to me a lot. But lately she's set up barriers."

Dom was alarmed by the implication. This, he was sure, was where the priest had been leading with his drive down memory lane.

"Do you think she should see a psychiatrist?"

"I wanted to talk to Kay about that. . . ."

"It's a hell of a time," Dom growled. Then, realizing he'd been overbrusque, he softened his tone. He couldn't refute the logic of the suggestion; and for Alice's sake, he couldn't afford to indulge his temper. "Can you imagine what Annie would do with that? She'd crucify the poor kid. I've seen what that woman can do."

Father Tom caught the unspoken agreement in his protests. "Don't worry about that," he smiled. "Kay can handle her."

The relentless ticking of the wipers marched across Dom's brooding silence as he weighed the oddly unfamiliar note of intimacy in Father Tom's assurances.

✠ ✠ ✠

Long after the door had buzzed open, the small figure in the yellow hooded raincoat kept pressing the button. She held her finger against the bell for another twenty seconds to make sure, then slipped into the empty hall. She took a mask from her shopping bag and adjusted it over her face before reaching for the knife.

Then she quickly opened the basement door, thrust the bag inside, and moved back to the foyer. She took a position at the base of the stairway and waited.

Except for the butcher knife protruding from her white-gloved fist, the figure resembled a shiny yellow ball as she crouched beneath the railing, smooth pink mask smiling patiently.

✠ ✠ ✠

The persistent buzz frayed Annie's temper.

"Who is it?" she shouted down the stairs, vainly pressing the button that unlocked the outside door.

The buzzing paused, then continued.

"If that's you, Alice, stop pushing that button!" Annie warned.

Catherine looked up sharply. "Maybe she simply locked herself out."

The anger barbing her calm tone deflated Annie's bluster. "I'll go down and open it," she sighed, pulling her coat off the hook. "May as well do some shopping since I'm going down anyway." She hesitated, then added, "Do you need anything, Kay?"

Catherine kept her back turned, unmoved by the apologetic offer. "No, thanks. But if it's Alice, please tell her that her special sandwich is ready."

✠ ✠ ✠

The figure crouched behind the base of the stairs stiffened at the first faint sound of footsteps above her.

The tinted plastic face hooded by the yellow St. Michael's slicker maintained its placid expression as she poised the knife between the spindles of the banister. Trembling with anticipation, she coiled her shoulder and listened intently as the footsteps became louder, trying to measure their rhythm.

Her timing was perfect. The first thrust speared an ankle just as it flashed into view.

Annie didn't see a thing until pain shivered through her leg. Frozen with shock, she gaped at the blood spreading across her shoe.

Then a yellow blur flicked through the slats and she jerked back, shrieking as the knife smacked her calf like a burning fist. Still screaming, Annie tried to scuttle back upstairs, but the constantly jabbing blade cut off her retreat.

She kicked spastically, screeching with terror as the knife relentlessly chewed at her shins, spraying the stairs with blood and bits of flesh.

Her foot skidded on a greasy splash of blood, and she lost her balance. As she fell the knife bit deep into her thigh and she flailed blindly with her purse.

The sudden realization that she was trapped clawed at Annie's throat as the hooded figure swung around the banister, mask leering hungrily.

"Don't, Alice . . . no . . . don't . . . help . . ." she squawked, eyes fixed on the blade lifting over her belly like a fat red tooth.

"What's going on? What's happening?"

The masked figure froze at Alphonso's alarmed whine. Then he loomed over the rail above them.

"Alice! It's Alice!" he squealed. "She's killing her aunt. She's killing Annie!"

Annie's vitality surged back when she saw the knife retract. The masked figure retreated swiftly to the door. She flung her purse at the hooded figure running into the hall and lurched after her.

Disregarding the agony searing her limbs, she staggered out to the rain-drenched street in frenzied pursuit. "I'll get you, Alice . . . I'll find you . . ." she squalled, lips frothing with hysterical rage as she reeled through the downpour searching for her niece.

Abruptly, Annie's legs refused to respond to her will and she collapsed, dumbly watching the bright streams of blood leaking into the gutter like red oil.

* * *

Alphonso was still shrieking down the empty stairwell when Catherine reached the second landing. "It's Alice. She's killing her!" he whined incessantly. "It's Alice!"

"Move, damn it! Move!" Catherine raged at the bloated hulk blocking the stairs.

Rushing outside, she saw her sister kneeling in a lake of blood. "Annie, what happened?" she yelled. As she neared, Annie twisted and lashed out wildly, fingers clawing for her face.

"Alice, get away from me! No, don't!"

Stunned, Catherine slapped her hard. The blow seemed to bring Annie around. She stopped struggling and stared at her sister. She tried to speak, but all that came out was a strangled croak before she fell into Catherine's arms, sobbing convulsively. Panicked by the gushing blood spreading across the rain-washed sidewalk, Catherine lost control.

"Help me!" she shrieked.

Her cry was drowned out by the rain drumming against the deserted street.

"Help me! Someone!" she cried out again. Desperately she tore a strip from Annie's skirt and pressed the cloth over her gashed legs, vainly trying to stem the flow of blood streaming across the concrete.

A car rounded the corner and she stood up, waving the blood-soaked cloth. Then she recognized Dom running toward her. His grim face bobbed nearer like a life raft, and she swam through the churning confusion to reach him.

"Oh, thank God! I can't stop the bleeding!" she babbled, pulling him toward Annie.

Dom took the cloth from her hand and knelt beside Annie. "Did anyone call an ambulance?"

Father Tom appeared behind him, and saw the wounds. "Let's get her into the car," he said. The three of them lifted Annie from the pavement. "Jesus Christ, what happened?" Dom grunted as they carried her to the car.

"Someone attacked her in the hallway."

"Has anyone called the police?"

Catherine grimaced impatiently. "How should I know?" She hurried ahead to open the car door.

"Careful, now, watch her legs," Father Tom murmured as they eased Annie into the back seat.

Annie leaned against the cushion and began moaning. "Jim . . . I want my Jim . . ."

"Don't worry, I'll call him," Dom said.

At the sound of his voice, Annie's eyes blinked open. "Dom, you find Alice," she croaked. "She tried to kill me. She's here somewhere. I was right behind her."

"Please stay calm," Catherine interrupted curtly, squeezing in beside her. "Everything will be all right—you need a doctor now."

Father Tom slipped behind the wheel. "Stay here, Dom. Call Jim. Tell him I'm taking her to the hospital."

"You find her," Annie whimpered as Dom shut the rear door. "She tried to kill me."

✠ ✠ ✠

Dom stood in the pouring rain until the car was out of sight before he turned back to the house. He walked slowly, following the pink ribbons of blood leading to the front door, then paused.

Annie's assailant certainly couldn't be in the house; this was the only exit. So she must have ducked into a hiding place.

Funny how he thought of the attacker as *she*, Dom thought bitterly. Annie's hysteria had him thinking of his little daughter as a homicidal maniac.

He moved back to the curb for a broader view of the area. Annie claimed that she'd been right behind the assailant, so whoever it was must have gone somewhere close by.

Scanning the buildings on both sides of the house, Dom saw that there were only three possible avenues of escape. Since Mr. Grimaldi's three-story house to the right was flush against Catherine's building, the only refuge there was through Grimaldi's front door.

The second possibility was the small Italian restaurant next to the Grimaldi house. It was closed, but the stacked garbage cans in front provided enough cover for a small person. He checked the restaurant first, searching behind—and even inside—the garbage cans. All he discovered was that Mama Ciardi used German noodles.

At the Grimaldi house, he gently tried the knob on the front door. Finger poised on the bell, Dom saw a glowing orb through the curtains. Recognizing Mrs. Grimaldi's portly outline in front of the TV set, Dom backed away. He hurried to the driveway separating Catherine's house from the bank on the other side. Since the bank was closed, the driveway was the only other escape route the attacker could have used.

Unfortunately it was virtually impossible to track. There was a yard behind the garage, and anyone could easily slip through the hedges to the yard beyond. Annie's assailant could be halfway across town by now. Although certain it was useless, Dom checked the garage before heading back to call Jim.

Dom was uncomfortably aware of the rain trickling under his collar as he walked down the driveway. Then he noticed something that made him forget about the weather.

The wooden door slanted against the side of the house was the fourth possibility—the one he'd overlooked. It led to the basement.

He started to lift the door, then paused. He'd be

defenseless if some maniac was hiding down there. There was another entrance to the basement in the front hall. The attacker most likely ducked in there before Annie could see her.

Dom stood uncertainly, rain dripping from his matted hair. If he used this entrance, he'd have to walk fifteen or twenty feet in total darkness to reach the light switch next to the laundry room.

The safest way would be to go around the front. There was a light switch just inside the door.

That might give the attacker time to get away, Dom decided, pulling the door open.

He stopped at the base of the stairs, until his vision adjusted to the gloom, then cautiously moved toward the laundry room.

After a few shuffling paces, the full realization of what he was doing brought him up short.

The killer could be in the laundry room—or behind the furnace—or under the stairs—or inside any of a dozen shadowy nooks waiting for him.

Given the darkness and the element of surprise, a little girl with a knife was as dangerous as a veteran commando.

There I go again, Dom noted angrily. *Still taking Annie's hysterical accusation as fact.* The guilt cut his hesitation, but not his caution.

Before proceeding to the laundry room, Dom edged to the storage bin. While the attacker could be lurking there, it wasn't probable. The piles of junk jammed inside the area made it a poor place to hide. However, it was an excellent place to scrounge up a weapon.

His tension fled when his fumbling hand clutched the handle of a coal shovel. Doubts squashed by its reassuring heft, Dom turned toward the laundry room.

A quick rustle yanked his head back and he froze, hands tight on the shovel.

He remained motionless for long seconds, eyes

straining through the darkness. Although reason told him that the sound was nothing more than a mouse, his bristling senses insisted that someone was waiting in the dense stillness.

Another swift rustle made him certain they were right. It sounded like fabric swishing the floor. But he couldn't pinpoint the source.

The first sound seemed to come from the furnace, but he could swear this one had come from the back of the bin.

Impossible, he thought. *The bin was completely crammed with old furniture and crated refuse. There wasn't room unless . . .*

He looked up, shovel poised.

Moron, he chided himself sheepishly, lowering his arms, *if anything heavier than a roach tried to climb that heap, it would collapse like a house of cards.*

The observation did nothing for his nerves as he peered into the shadowy mass, still puzzling over the sound's direction.

He moved deeper into the bin, back pressed against the wall, and the shovel shielding his neck.

Then he saw the light. Incredulously, Dom watched the glimmer dart between the stacked crates like an insect.

Shovel ready to strike, he stepped closer to the crates.

"Don't take me, Karen. I swear to God I didn't steal it!"

The shrill cry snapped Dom's coiled reflexes. He sprang forward, thrust the shovel into a narrow space outlined by the flickering light, and used the handle to pry the space apart.

As the space widened, he saw Alice kneeling on the floor, swollen eyes shimmering madly beneath the dancing candle flame.

"I was saving it for you, Karen. You can have it!" Alice quavered.

She lifted her hands.

"Take it, Karen."

There was a doll cradled in her upraised palms. Alice's rigid grimace was covered by the doll's weeping, porcelain face, as it extended toward him.

"Alice, it's me. It's Daddy," Dom whispered, arms stretching warily, as if about to awaken a cobra.

The doll fell away from her blank, bloodless face, and she scrambled to him.

"Daddy, Daddy, help me—please help me!" Alice babbled, clinging to him fiercely. "I never meant for her to die. I didn't want Karen to die!"

"It's all right, Daddy's here. No one's going to hurt you. It's okay," he crooned, arms muffling the spasms jerking through her stiff limbs.

Dom held her close for a long time while his numbed gaze roamed over the photograph, prayerbook, icepick, and jar of cockroaches, neatly arranged on the bureau. He knew she was his daughter and he loved her dearly, but he couldn't understand what Alice had become—or what he'd done to make her that way.

7

Father Tom smiled hopefully as Catherine left the phone booth. "Everything all right?"

"Yes," she said quickly, her eyes betraying the lie.

"Was she in the cellar the whole time?"

She didn't seem to hear. "Oh, Tom, who's doing this to me? Haven't I been through enough?"

"Kay—hold yourself together."

She glanced around the hospital lobby then lowered her voice. "Yes . . . but Alphonso . . ."

Her eyes filled with tears. "Alphonso told the police it was Alice. They're on their way."

"Did he actually see her?"

"Of course not!" Catherine snapped. "How could he? He's just repeating what he heard Annie scream. Don't you see? People believe what they want to believe."

"What's important is how the police will look at these things," Tom reminded softly.

She looked away. "They don't know her. No one knows her like I do. What—what if Annie tells them—what she told us?"

"We have to wait and see what happens."

She glanced up at him. "What can they do, Tom? Can they take her away?" Sudden desperation flashed across her face. "I won't let them do that. She's no murderer. She'd never hurt anyone."

"Of course not, Kay," Father Tom murmured, holding her arm. "But if the police have good enough reason, they will take her in for questioning. Once they talk to Annie, they may have enough reason." He paused, making sure she understood. "You've got to be prepared for that."

Catherine misinterpreted his advice. "I'll tell them Annie was hysterical," she said grimly. "When I got there, she didn't even know me. She never would have said such a thing if she hadn't been in shock."

Before he could dissuade her, Tom saw a stocky man in a wrinkled blue suit enter the hospital lobby. Ignoring the nurse at the front desk, the man walked toward them.

Tom didn't change expression. "Kay, Detective Beame is here," he warned calmly.

"I've got to talk to Annie," she hissed. "Give me a minute."

She turned and walked quickly to the elevators, giving Tom no choice but to try to stall Beame.

✠ ✠ ✠

A horde of seething resentments tumbled through Catherine's brain as she hurried down the corridor to Annie's ward.

Since childhood Annie had been burying her in guilt. Her constant sniping at Dom hadn't been the most insignificant factor in their breakup. And now she wanted to take Alice as well.

She'd been too weak all her life, Catherine reflected bitterly. Annie's domination had already cost too much.

Alice had been born six months after she and Dom were married, and Annie never let them forget. That was the real reason she resented Alice so much.

Catherine knew she should have listened to Dom and moved away from her sister's influence, but she'd lacked the courage to try. Instead, she'd allowed Annie to poison her marriage with constant recriminations.

This time, however, she intended to fight to protect Alice from her aunt's hate.

When Catherine pulled aside the curtain walling off her sister's bed, Annie shut her eyes, pretending to be asleep.

"Annie," she whispered urgently. "It's me. Please wake up."

Catherine stared intently at her sister's mute, stony features. "I want to talk to you."

There was no response, but she went on. "I know you won't do this to me. You can't do it, Annie. You didn't realize what you were saying. How could you? You were too upset."

Annie turned away, tears streaming from her closed eyes.

"Don't turn away like that. What's wrong with you? Have you gone crazy?"

A cluster of approaching footsteps ignited Catherine's desperation. "I swear on Momma . . . I swear on our mother's soul . . . that I'll never forgive you," she warned, voice hoarse.

The nurse pulled the curtain back.

"How are you feeling, Mrs. Lorenzi?" she asked cheerfully. "Dr. Barnet says it's okay to talk to Captain Beame."

Annie looked up and saw Father Tom. "Where's my Jim? Didn't you call him?"

"He's on his way," Tom assured.

Beame gave Catherine a cordial nod, then turned to Annie. "I won't keep you long. But you know it's important that I talk to you."

Annie nodded, tears trickling down her pinched face.

"Do you think you can tell us what happened, Mrs. Lorenzi?"

Although surprised when Annie glared at her sister in tight-lipped silence, Beame retained his bland tone. "It's important for us to know exactly what you saw."

She didn't answer, her eyes locked on her sister.

Tensed perceptions concealed behind an apologetic smile, Beame glanced at Father Tom.

"Father, do you mind? Could you and Mrs. Spages please go out for a few minutes?"

Catherine stiffened. "After all, I'm her sister. And I was there, too."

"Of course, Mrs. Spages. And I want to hear everything you can tell me," Beame assured. "I'll be with you in a few minutes."

His steely politeness discouraged further argument. Resigned, Catherine allowed Tom to pull her away from the bed.

As they emerged from the curtains, however, Jim burst into the ward and rushed toward them. "What happened? Where's Annie?" he stammered.

"Jim? Oh, Jimmy!"

At Annie's wail, Jim spun away from Father Tom and rushed to his wife's side, moaning as they embraced. "I was so worried. They said that someone tried to kill you."

"Oh my God, it was awful," Annie bawled. "She stabbed, and stabbed . . . my legs . . . my feet . . ."

"Who? Who did this?"

"Annie, be careful!" Catherine warned.

" . . . stabbing and stabbing . . . she wanted to kill me," Annie sobbed. "Oh my God, I don't believe it."

Catherine moved closer to the bed. "Annie. Shut up."

"For Christ's sake, Kay, let her talk," Jim sputtered. His small eyes darted from Catherine to the unfamiliar figure behind Father Tom.

"What's going on here?" he demanded, his face twitching like a plump, outraged rabbit.

Though disappointed that he'd been noticed, Captain Beame was still hopeful. He sensed the old shrew was on the verge of singing. His optimism expanded at her shrill self-righteous protest.

"I love her, Catherine. She's like my own flesh."

"You do not. You hate her. You hate Alice!" Catherine lashed back.

Annie lurched off her pillow, arms extended toward Father Tom in shocked appeal. "It's not true. May God strike me dead if I'm lying!"

Jim tried to push her back. "Don't, Annie, please! What are you saying?"

"Liar! You're all liars!" Catherine ranted, struggling against Father Tom's restraining arm. "Face it, Anna . . . face it! You want to believe it was Alice." She twisted suddenly and confronted Beame.

"Why not Angela? She wasn't in the church."

Her accusation smothered the noise like a glove. Beame scowled glumly, unable to answer.

"You see? You see?" Catherine cried triumphantly.

When Beame looked away, her triumph collapsed. "Oh, Tom, what are they trying to do? Can't you see?" she whimpered, her body sagging in the priest's arms.

Beame studied the couple for long, reflective moments before moving to the phone.

✠ ✠ ✠

Detective Lieutenant Michael Spina inspected the neatly tagged evidence on his desk with gloating satisfaction. They'd cracked more than a tough case. This one would crack a few headlines.

He lifted the prayerbook, scanned the desk, and picked up the icepick with his other hand.

This would make a great shot, he mused, extending the objects toward an imaginary camera. A magazine spread might boost him all the way to the DA's office.

Spina was still pondering whether the doll or the prayerbook would look best with the icepick when Cranston finally arrived.

The tall, thin man scowled at Spina. "What the hell's goin' on? It was like flies greeting shit when I came in." He parked his black metal suitcase on a chair and unbuttoned his coat.

"You're late," Spina murmured.

"Ray knows it's my day off," Cranston barked.

Spina leaned back, his smile heavy with sympathy. Cranston's prim features and conservative gray suit made him look more like a mortician than a cop, but he was tough. And Spina needed him to nail this case shut.

"It's an unusual situation," he confided. "I hope you're prepared to test a twelve-year-old girl."

Cranston's gaping mouth revealed that he wasn't. "Who?"

"Remember the girl killed in the church last Sunday, Karen Spages? Her sister Alice tried to stick a butcher knife in her aunt this afternoon."

"Then what the hell do you need me for?"

"Our esteemed superior Captain Beame won't book her until he's absolutely sure." Spina gestured disgustedly at the evidence arrayed on the desk. "Even with eyewitness testimony and all this, he needs a polygraph expert."

He rolled his eyes upward, hands clasped in mock prayer. "Papa Beame's got a soft spot for little girls."

Mood deflated by the barbed truth behind the joke, Spina snatched a sheet of paper from his typewriter. "Here's a list of questions they agreed to. Let's get up there before Papa blows a fuse."

When they reached the interrogation room, Spina pointed out the suspect through the one-way window. As Cranston studied Alice Spages, his professional detachment was diluted by sympathy. The homely little girl sitting between Beame and her parents seemed dazed with terror. Like a lost puppy.

If she killed her sister, the brat had good reason to be scared, Cranston grimly reminded himself, moving to the door of the interrogation room.

Beame was the only one who seemed happy to see him. The parents nodded when the captain introduced Cranston, and nervously watched him unlock the suitcase; but the little girl never looked at the equipment. She kept her eyes on Cranston's face as he set up the machine.

Satisfied the graph was in order, Cranston nodded to Beame.

"If you don't mind, Mrs. Spages," the detective murmured. "He's ready."

They rose and hovered protectively around their daughter, unwilling to leave her.

"We'll be right next door," Dom whispered. "Do exactly what Captain Beame told you."

"Don't worry, everything will be fine," Catherine added, giving her a hug before following Dom to the door.

After they'd gone, Cranston smiled at Alice. "I guess Captain Beame explained how this works," he said gently. "But I'll explain it again to make sure." He picked up the pliable contact tube and leaned over her. "Just lift your arms—this won't hurt."

Alice didn't flinch. "I know all about it," she hissed. "And I'm not afraid."

Cranston didn't need the polygraph to tell him it was true.

Outside, Dom and Catherine watched through the one-way mirror, unable to hear what was being said as Cranston adjusted the tube around Alice. When he switched on the machine, his voice crackled through the outside speakers.

"Remember," Cranston said, picking up a stack of cards. "You're to answer no to every card. I *want* you to lie."

He held up a card. "Is it the three?"

"No."

He held up another. "Is it the six?"

"No," Alice repeated woodenly.

Annoyed, Catherine turned to Beame. "Why does that man want her to lie?"

The detective gave her an apologetic shrug. "That's how they test the machine."

"That's it. Thank you, Alice," Cranston said, shuffling the cards and putting them aside. Then he added casually, "The first one was the three, wasn't it?"

Alice hesitated. "Yes. The three."

"Okay, it's working," Cranston droned, checking the graph at her truthful answer. "Well, now, let's get to the questions. Okay?"

Sensing she'd been tricked, Alice nodded, warily eying the machine beside him.

"Do you intend to answer truthfully to every question?"

She nodded again.

"Please just answer yes or no," Cranston prompted.

"Yes."

"Do you know for sure who stabbed your aunt?"

"No."

Cranston's voice remained impassive as the graph lines shivered, indicating a lie.

"Did you stab your aunt?"

The polygraph's placid waves showed that Alice was telling the truth.

"During your entire life, did you ever deliberately hurt someone who trusted you?"

She looked from Cranston to the polygraph beside him. "I—I—put Angela's coat in the toilet. But I didn't lie! I told sister I did it," Alice declared, staring at the machine as if expecting it to forgive her.

"In the suitcase we found in your basement were a white dress and a mask. Are they yours?"

Her gaze flicked back like a switchblade. "Yes."

Cranston had tested everything from Mafia chieftains to an ax-murderess who stored her husband's chopped remains in her refrigerator—but something about the little girl's expression spooked him.

The polygraph results on his next series of questions unnerved Cranston completely.

"Did you stab your aunt with a knife this afternoon at three o'clock?"

"No."

The needle flickered, indicating severe stress.

"Are you deliberately withholding information about the attack on your aunt?"

"No."

The needle jumped again.

"Do you know who stabbed your aunt?"

"No!"

The needle leaped past the stress line at her lie.

"Do you know who stabbed your aunt?" he repeated sharply.

"Yes! Yes! It was Karen!" She jerked her head

to the machine. "No one believes me. Karen stabbed Aunt Annie!"

Incredulously, Cranston stared at the serenely bobbing lines on the graph that testified Alice was telling the truth.

* * *

After escorting Alice's parents to his office, Detective Spina hurried back to the interrogation room with high anticipation.

Beame didn't look up when he entered. "Any word from the boys?" he grunted, still watching the girl and Cranston through the window.

"They're still combing the grounds."

"Sure wish they could find that knife."

Spina didn't answer, unwilling to let Beame's negativism dampen his hopes. However, the contrite expression that clouded Cranston's expression as he left the interrogation room seemed like a storm warning. The polygraph expert looked at Beame and shrugged. "I don't know what to tell you."

"Well, for Christ's sake, did she fail or didn't she?" Spina rumbled impatiently.

Cranston scratched his head. "*Technically,* I guess she failed."

"Well, I guess that nails it," Spina said briskly.

"Easy now, Mike." Beame squinted at the lie-detector specialist. "What does that mean—*technically* she failed?"

Cranston became defensive. "Look. I asked if she knew who stabbed her aunt. She lied. She said no. Then I asked her again. She said it was her sister. But her sister is dead." He lowered his voice. "Only thing is, this time she wasn't lying. So what do you want from me? The kid is off the wall."

Beame sighed and turned away.

"You've got to hold her, Ray," Spina warned. "If not for the murder, for the stabbing of her aunt. Let the psychiatrists give us some answers."

Beame examined the tips of his shoes as if he'd stepped into something unpleasant.

"All right. Call Mary to stay with her while I talk to her parents."

As he wearily headed for the door and Spina grabbed the phone, Cranston wandered to the observation window.

Alice sat at the end of the table, watching the polygraph machine.

She was either crazy, or the most diabolical mind he'd ever encountered, Cranston decided, trying to exorcise his lingering uneasiness. But even if the kid was sane, she could still scare hell out of any adult with her strange intensity.

"Have Mary get up to interrogation right away," Spina barked, behind him.

Cranston glanced back. "She's a weird little girl—that's sure. Did you notice her tits?"

Spina shook his head, but his expression reflected deep interest.

"When I put the tube around her, she looked at me as if I was feeling her up."

He was cut off by a quick movement at the corner of his vision. Cranston whirled and saw the little girl edging around the table, hands extended toward the lie-detector.

"Hey, stop it, you damned bitch—stop!" he raged, pounding uselessly at the soundproof window.

Alice looked up calmly, as if able to see him through the mirror on her side of the one-way glass. Then she reached out and swept the machine off the table.

Cranston was still yelling, as he watched the polygraph smash silently to the floor.

8

The monsignor was having his usual lunchtime tantrum. He rocked impatiently in his wheelchair as Father Pat, the assistant pastor of St. Michael's parish, rolled him to the head of the table.

"Now, now," Father Pat said gently, "Mrs. Tredoni wants you to eat with us today."

The rotund priest beamed at her as he sat down, then mumbled a hasty prayer and attacked his breaded cutlet with relish. Across from him, Mrs. Tredoni methodically cut the monsignor's veal into tiny pieces.

"I'm not feeling well," the old man sniffled. "Tell the children to stay out."

"You know I don't let any children into the house," Mrs. Tredoni said wearily. She slid the plate in front of him, then pressed a fork against his palsied palm.

"Do you want me to feed you, or can you manage by yourself?"

"I'm not dead yet," the old man sputtered as the fork fell from his trembling fingers.

"It's all right. I'll help you," Mrs. Tredoni said tonelessly. She wiped the fork clean and lifted a piece of veal to the monsignor's lips. "Isn't Father Tom coming to lunch?" she asked Pat.

The balding young priest gave her a sympathetic glance. "He went down to the courthouse this morning. The Spages case."

"He needs to eat," Mrs. Tredoni declared, her craggy features fixed in an indignant scowl.

"It's a very delicate matter," Father Pat assured. "But I'm sure he'll be here soon."

"And everything will be ice-cold," Mrs. Tredoni sighed.

"Well, hot or cold, I'm sure he'll find it's delicious. You're a wonder of a cook, Mrs. Tredoni."

The monsignor looked up. "Cold? Cold? No. She's a good woman. Tell him not to worry."

"More coffee?" Mrs. Tredoni asked, ignoring the demented remarks.

Father Pat pushed his plate aside. "No, thanks. I've got to get over to the school. I've got children's mass this Sunday."

"Where's my Sanka?" the Monsignor demanded, averting his face from Mrs. Tredoni's fork.

"I only have two hands, monsignor," she snapped. Her annoyance escalated when she heard the doorbell.

"Where's my Sanka!" the old man croaked, as she rose to answer the door.

"I'll get it," Father Pat said. "Take care of His Eminence. It's probably Father Tom."

Mrs. Tredoni dropped gratefully into her chair. Father Pat was a good man. Even with his important position, he was never too proud to help with a simple task.

Not like this peacock, she reflected acidly, pouring hot water into the monsignor's cup. Even before the stroke, he behaved more like a feudal lord than a servant of Jesus.

"I want my cake!" he simpered.

She ignored him, curious to hear who was at the door. The sound of Dominic Spages dug a deep furrow between her narrowed eyes. That family brought nothing but trouble. Father Tom had already missed lunch twice because of them.

"I want my cake now!"

Exasperated, Mrs. Tredoni swept the plate of meat aside and pushed the dessert in front of the old man.

She rapidly shoveled the shortcake into his mouth, determined to keep the monsignor quiet while she listened.

Father Pat saw the glum faces on Father Tom and Dom Spages when they entered.

"How did it go?" he inquired mildly.

Father Tom shrugged.

"Just as we expected," Dom said. "The judge ruled that she be held for psychiatric observation."

"Don't lose hope," Pat said, automatically reaching for his coat. "How's Catherine taking it?"

A flicker of pride lightened Dom's frown. "Even the lawyer was amazed at her strength."

Happy he'd struck a hopeful note, Father Pat buttoned his coat. "Ralph's a good man," he assured. "From the way people talk, you've got one of the best criminal lawyers around." He walked to the door. "Good luck!"

"Thanks for covering me this morning, Pat," Father Tom called as he left. Then he turned and rummaged through the silence for some way to ease his friend's pain.

"Any way to appeal it?" he asked, guiding Dom into the living room.

"Not this. The lawyer said it was mandatory."

His next suggestion was interrupted by a choked burst of coughing from the next room. Father Tom went to the door and saw Mrs. Tredoni wiping off the gobs of cream spattered across the monsignor's cassock.

"Do you want lunch, Father Tom?" she asked hopefully.

"Not right now, thanks." He raised his voice. "Hello, monsignor."

The old man looked up. Half his face was crumpled like a wad of paper, paralyzed by the stroke. But the vital side beamed happily at his protégé.

"Monsignor, you remember Dominic Spages," Father Tom continued in a clear, loud voice.

The old prelate returned his attention to a dab of cream on his finger.

Dom looked questioningly at Father Tom.

"It's all right. He's not really cogent since his illness. Have a seat. I'll get you the information you wanted. Mrs. Tredoni, would you get Mr. Spages some coffee?"

As Father Tom left the room, the old man slowly lifted his head. "I can't see anyone today," he quavered. "I gave strict orders."

"Monsignor, this is Mr. Spages. He's waiting for Father Tom," Mrs. Tredoni droned loudly.

The monsignor nodded. "Mrs. Spages, yes . . . a good woman. . . ." His palsied fingers brushed the crucifix at his chest. "God bless all the good women . . . all . . ." He peered at Dom. "Did you know her?"

"Monsignor, this is her husband," Mrs. Tredoni said sharply. "I offer my prayers for her," she added as she poured coffee into Dom's cup.

Her grim piety discouraged Dom from reminding Mrs. Tredoni that he'd divorced Catherine and was no longer her husband.

"Prayers . . . yes, prayers . . ." the old man mumbled. "Ask her to pray for me."

Mrs. Tredoni grunted apologetically. "The mind is gone, but the heart is as strong as ever, thank the Lord."

Dom was relieved when Tom entered, waving a sheaf of papers. "These are the order sheets. I called Mother Superior's commissary, and she has all the names and addresses of everyone who purchased the coats."

Dom tucked the list into his pocket. "Angela has one of these coats, doesn't she?"

Father Tom measured the desperation behind the calm question. "Easy, now," he said gently. "You're groping. Do you realize how many kids have these coats?"

"Look, they didn't find the knife or Karen's cross with the other things in the basement. Angela wasn't in the church when Karen was killed. All of that's pure fact. Now Alice said she saw Karen in her school coat. She must have seen someone—even if it wasn't Angela. And whoever it is might be on that purchase list."

"And if this lead doesn't work, how long will you stay around and play detective?"

Dom's smile was a thin crack in a granite wall. "I'm staying as long as it takes to find Karen's murderer."

He stood up and buttoned his coat. "Thanks for your help. I appreciate your letting me borrow the car. I'll drop it off tomorrow."

"Keep it as long as you need it," Father Tom said, accompanying him to the door.

As their voices faded into the hall, the monsignor pushed away from the table.

"Tomorrow? Never!" he declared, hands flapping angrily against the sides of the wheelchair. "I don't want that girl in my house. She can't talk to St. Michael!"

✠ ✠ ✠

The Sarah Reed Children's Center reminded Dom of an army base as he drove toward the front gate.

To Catherine, the sprawling complex of drab concrete buildings seemed like a barren purgatory for her failure as a mother.

To Dr. Whitman, the institution's resident psychiatrist, the center was a temple to the only deity she recognized—the human mind. And she was its priestess.

This profound sense of mission illuminated Dr. Whitman's maternal features as she intoned the results of her test session into a Dictaphone.

"Subject: Alice Spages. Twelve years, one month, normal physical development, no apparent physical defects. Subject is a suspicious, hostile adolescent, especially toward an aunt with whom she stayed during a trial separation of her parents. Subject represses hostilities toward her mother and estranged father. Jealousy of dead sister neutralized in role imitation."

Dr. Whitman swiveled in her leather armchair, her blue eyes glazed with reflection as they wandered over the framed diplomas, professional awards, and civil endorsements adorning the wall.

"Strong indications of schizoid personality. Subject is capable of extremely violent action. Note cunning antisocial behavior, as per school records. Product of broken yet orthodox Catholic home. This factor could be extremely significant and suggests—"

Her judgment was suspended by a knock at the door. Filing a mental note to expand the last entry, Dr. Whitman switched off the Dictaphone.

"Come in."

"Mr. and Mrs. Spages are here," the nurse announced.

"Show them in, please."

Dr. Whitman observed the couple who approached her desk without enthusiasm. Typical and predictable. He the popular image of the blond, masculine, upwardly mobile executive; and she the typical wife, bound by religious guilts to tribe and family. Of course they were divorced, and of course they'd be hostile.

"Just sit anywhere," she chirped with well-trained cordiality. "I had a session with Alice this morning, and I thought I ought to talk to you before your visit with her."

"Is something wrong?" Catherine asked sharply.

Dr. Whitman deflected the question with a placid smile. "It's far too soon to make any conclusions. As understaffed as we are, we strive to give all the children as much time as they would get in private practice," she added, the note of harried pride directed at Dom.

He made no effort to conceal his dislike. "I think you should know that my lawyer is doing all he can to get Alice home with her mother."

"That's what I wanted to warn you about. I wouldn't encourage Alice to believe that you'll be taking her home soon." The authority steeling Dr. Whitman's tone softened. "Perhaps being home with her mother isn't the best thing."

The solemn pronouncement had no effect on Dom's stony scowl, but Catherine's face crumbled.

"What do you mean?"

Dr. Whitman clasped her hands. "Be prepared for hostility from Alice," she confided gravely. "At this point, it's only natural for her to hold you responsible for her predicament. She's nursing an inordinate amount of anger and resentment which stems from a rather negative self-image." She glanced sympathetically at Catherine. "You might say that like all of us, she blames others for her troubles."

"Well, isn't that normal?" Catherine challenged. "It doesn't take a genius to understand how Alice feels. A lot of people she trusted are responsible for putting her in here."

Dr. Whitman sighed regretfully. "Alice has many deep-seated problems."

"But she's no murderess," Catherine reminded coldly.

Perceiving that her primitive obstinacy made further explanations useless, Dr. Whitman's smile faded. "She needs psychological help. That's my decision."

Dom nodded. "I assume there are no objections to our working with our own psychiatrist?"

Dr. Whitman wasn't duped by the mild question. Mr. Spages obviously had been well coached by his lawyer and knew the answer in advance.

"Not at all—it's your right," Dr. Whitman said sweetly. "But I'm sure you're anxious to see Alice now." She buzzed for the nurse and stood up. "Let me remind you to be candid about the issue of going home. Be assured she'll get the best possible treatment here."

The nurse opened the door.

"Take the Spages to the living room," Dr. Whitman said, returning to her Dictaphone.

They were almost at the door when she looked up. "Oh, Mrs. Spages."

As Catherine turned, Dr. Whitman regarded her with a pensive smile. "Why would Alice conceal from you the fact that she's begun menstruating?"

Catherine's mouth jerked open like a hooked fish. She gaped helplessly, unable to answer.

"It never ceases to amaze me how often parents don't know their children as well as they presume," Dr. Whitman mused.

Catherine stared in stunned silence until Dom pulled her from the room.

✠ ✠ ✠

When the nurse left the center's living room to fetch Alice, Catherine exploded. "You've got to do something about that woman! I don't trust her. All that stuff about taking her time. She's already made up her mind."

"Don't get upset. Not now," Dom said softly. "If she knew anything, she wouldn't be working in this place. For God's sake, trust me. Our psychiatrist will be here tomorrow."

He set the suitcase packed with Alice's things beside the sofa and looked around. A few crayon drawings Scotch-taped to the wall did little to relieve the austerity of the drably furnished room.

Catherine wandered to the window, clutching the brown paper bag she'd brought for Alice over her heart like a shield. Abruptly, she whirled. "I don't care what they do with the wall," she said vehemently. "They can never make it look like somebody's living room."

Dom nodded glumly. She was right. No one had ever lived here. "I wonder how many kids they have," he said, tugging at the knob.

An unexpected pang of anguish pierced his question when he discovered the door was locked from the outside. He glanced back and saw Catherine's wide-eyed desolation as she, too, realized that they were in a prison.

The scratch of the key in the lock startled them. Silently, they watched the door open and Alice enter.

She stopped just inside, eyes dull and sullen. The nurse loomed behind her. "When you're finished with your visit, just ring the bell."

As the door clicked shut, both Dom and Catherine instinctively moved toward Alice, then hesitated; held back by the hostility veiling her expression.

"They said I could visit your room," Catherine said brightly. "I bet it's real nice."

"I hear they even have a swimming pool," Dom added.

Alice glared past him. "Why did you bring the big suitcase? Aren't you taking me home?"

"Not until the doctor says you're ready."

Alice angrily stalked across the room to the sofa. When her mother sat beside her, she edged away.

Catherine pretended she didn't notice. "What did you and the doctor talk about?" she asked gently.

"A lot of things."

Dom knelt in front of her. "Like what, Ally?" he urged.

Her lips curled back defiantly. "I told her Aunt Annie lies." Contempt chilled her voice as she turned to Catherine. "And you let her lie."

"But that's not true."

Alice ignored her mother's pained outburst. "What's in the bag?"

Catherine tried to smile. "I thought you'd like some of your things."

"Why? Don't you want me to come home?" Alice sneered. "You and Aunt Annie and that slob Alphonso . . . you just want to keep me here."

"Alice, you're hurting your mother. I don't want to hear you talk like that."

She responded to Dom's gentle reproof with a mocking laugh. "How would you like to hear what Aunt Annie says about you?"

Dom shrugged. "Someday you'll learn to ignore people like that."

"You don't have to worry. Daddy will find out the real truth." Catherine reached tentatively to stroke her hair, but Alice drew away.

"How can he? He has to go home . . . to his wife."

Dom gripped her shoulders. "I promise you, Ally. I'm going to stay until I find whoever was in that hall with your aunt."

The promise melted some of her antagonism. "But I don't want to stay in this place. Why can't I come home?"

"Court order. The judge says you must stay until your medical tests are finished."

"Medical tests!" Alice snorted. "She's a *psychiatrist*. Everyone thinks I'm crazy because I said it was Karen." She pulled away.

"And you don't believe me either."

Dom searched his daughter's icy face for a spark of trust. "Can you understand that there are two different reasons why you're here? One of them is because your aunt was attacked while you were in the basement."

He smiled and lowered his voice, as if sharing a secret. "We know you didn't do it. And I'll find out who did. Do you understand?"

"Yes, but. . ."

Sensing he was close to reaching her Dom pressed on. "The other reason is because you saw Karen. Now that can't be so. And with the help of a doc—a psychiatrist, I mean—we'll straighten that out, too. But it may take time."

"I *did* see Karen." The hollow finality in her voice told Dom she was far away again. Then he heard the door open and knew he'd lost her.

The nurse stepped inside. "I'm sorry, but time's almost up. Dr. Whitman would like to see you before she leaves."

"Somebody has to take my suitcase into my room," Alice demanded, arms folded.

As Dom reached for the suitcase, Catherine touched his arm.

"You go ahead. I'll meet you outside. I can handle the suitcase."

Suddenly understanding, Dom set it down and embraced Alice tightly. "I know I can rely on my Ally," he whispered.

* * *

Catherine struggled to suppress her dismay when she entered Alice's cramped, cell-like room. With forced enthusiasm she swung the suitcase onto the gray metal cot and snapped the lid open.

"Shall I help you put your things away?"

"No—I want to leave—I'll do it later," Alice said, digging into the brown paper bag.

Crestfallen by the curt refusal, Catherine slowly lowered the lid. "I packed your heavy robe—just in case."

"I don't need it."

Catherine cast about wildly for a way to prolong their privacy.

"Oh. The little radio is in there, too. Now, don't stay up all hours listening to it."

Alice remained intent on a hand puppet she'd found in the paper bag.

"I can't. I'm not allowed."

"I guess they want to make sure you get your rest," Catherine said weakly.

The inane remark consumed her last shred of hope. "I'd better go. But I'll be back tomorrow."

Alice didn't look up.

Suddenly Catherine knelt down and embraced her. "Oh, Alice, you know I love you, don't you?" she pleaded.

"I suppose so," Alice sighed dutifully.

"You'll be on my mind every minute, dear," Catherine crooned, kissing her over and over. Then she tore herself away and hurried to the door, emotions tottering.

"Why did you bring this puppet? You know I can't play with it anymore."

The petulant accusation seemed to restore Catherine's balance. She smiled sheepishly as she took the puppet from Alice's extended hand, grateful for the extra few seconds.

"I'll take it back. I'm sorry. I keep forgetting how old you are."

Alice glowered in silent resentment.

Catherine restrained herself from looking back as she pressed the bell for the nurse until her daughter's frenzied cry shattered all control.

"Don't go, Mommy! Don't leave me! I'm frightened! I don't want to be alone here. I need you!"

Exhilaration surged through Catherine's being as she swept Alice into her arms, weeping in joy and despair.

"I need *you*, baby. You're my whole world. I have no one but you."

Alice's voice was soft and very distant. "I'm so awful. How can you love me?"

"Oh, Alice, Alice, don't you ever say such a thing," she whispered fiercely.

She cupped her daughter's face between her hands, her eyes glowing. "Nobody will hurt us. You'll see, darling, everything's going to be perfect again. Just you wait and see."

9

If she stood on a certain spot on the old suspension bridge spanning the Passaic Falls, and faced just so, it was possible to glimpse a ghost of the waterfall's virgin majesty; before industry cut away the forests, and corrupted the river into a wasted whore.

Catherine wondered what the world was like before divorces and psychiatrists and prisons for little girls as she gazed down at the mist-clouded rocks. Were people happier then, perhaps kinder to each other? Or had life always been so empty?

Dom waited in the car with a container of coffee, unwilling to brave the cold, wet wind above the falls. As he watched Catherine's solitary outline lean over the rail, the sudden awareness of her mood touched a nerve.

Alarmed by the intuition, he left the car and hurried to the bridge.

When he reached Catherine, she was still leaning over the rail as if searching the rocks below for something she'd lost.

"Aren't you cold?" he said softly.

She seemed not to hear. "It's beautiful, isn't it, Dom?"

"You always liked this place."

Dom buttoned his raincoat and joined her at the rail. Hands jammed into his pockets, he watched the swirling yellow water until the chill became unbearable.

"You must be freezing," he scolded, pulling Catherine away from the rail. "Time to go back."

Spurred by the cold, he broke into a trot. "Come on, slowpoke."

"Who's a slowpoke?" she yelled, running past him toward the car.

Dom let her win and was rewarded by a breathless fit of giggling that washed the pain from her face. She was young again, glowing with the mischievous exuberance of the girl who'd been his high-school sweetheart. Magically, the years were gone, and nothing had changed.

Dom was the first to break the long, awkward silence.

"Better drink some of this coffee."

Catherine accepted the container, both hands cradling it for warmth as she watched him take a pack of cigarettes from his coat, then rummage through his clothes for a match.

"Try your shirt."

Her playful suggestion charged another familiar circuit between them.

"Never have learned," Dom grinned, pulling the matches from his shirt pocket.

Catherine smiled but didn't answer. She contemplated the coffee container in her hands as the silence thickened and then, almost without realizing asked, "Are you happy?"

Dom seemed startled. He took a deep drag on

his cigarette before answering. "As happy as anyone can be, I guess. Are you happy?"

"Did you talk to Julia today?"

The mention of his second wife made Dom uncomfortable. "I spoke to her this morning."

"How is she?"

"Don't change the subject. I asked you: Are you happy?"

"I guess I've been content. Until now."

"Are you seeing anyone special?"

"No one special."

Dom was disappointed, knowing the small blow to his male ego would ease much of his guilt.

"It must of been hard on you and the kids. . . ."

"Not really. But I keep wondering if Alice might have . . ." She shrugged off the thought with a rueful smile. "Guess I haven't been a howling success as a father and mother."

"I should have visited more often," he insisted.

"You were busy, Dom . . . with all the traveling . . . and Julia. . . ."

He gripped the wheel as he felt the old resentments rise. "Damn it, Kay, let's not try to fool each other now. I stopped coming long before the divorce. I felt you wanted me to clear out."

"I guess I was selfish," Catherine said acidly. "I didn't realize how much Alice needed her father."

Dom shook his head in bewilderment. "I never understood what you were so afraid of. You put up an iron curtain. It's no sin to enjoy sex with your husband."

"Maybe I felt I was holding you back from what you really wanted."

"I loved you, Catherine."

She flinched and looked away quickly.

"You made it so easy for me to leave," he sighed. "Almost as if you wanted it more than I did."

"I could never fit into the mold you had in mind," Catherine said, face still averted.

"You were afraid to try."

Stung by his accusation, Catherine turned to tell him all the agonizing ways she had tried. The talks with her doctor, the secretive discussions with her friends, the hormone pills, even a furtive, soul-wrenching trek to a dingy bookstore in New York, that sold pornography under the counter. She'd tried and tried until it was clear that her lonely crusade was a lost cause.

But when she met his eyes, her anger faded with the realization that he'd never understand what it was like for her. To Dom it was all so simple: a woman was supposed to be a saint before the ceremony and a nymphomaniac after.

"Perhaps you're right," she conceded tonelessly. "Anyway . . . it's one way to look at it."

Dom seemed troubled by the comment.

She leaned closer and smiled. "I'll bet you're starved."

He grinned. "How'd you guess? Hear my stomach growl, perchance?"

Catherine gave him a look of utter disdain. "Take me home, James," she sniffed. "Her royal highness feels like cooking."

✠ ✠ ✠

It was a fine dinner, and afterward as they sat together on the couch, lingering over their coffee, both Catherine and Dom were aware of a new bond of intimacy. They'd become friends during these few quiet hours; something they'd never been during their marriage.

But when Dom revealed his plan, Catherine's resistance flared immediately.

"It doesn't make sense," she said flatly.

Dom folded his arms and sighed. "Why couldn't it be Angela?"

"For one thing, Annie's her own mother."

"I can't believe that kid has any great love for Annie," Dom snorted. "I'll find out tomorrow if she was in school during the stabbing."

Wordlessly, Catherine left the couch and walked into the bedroom. She returned with a yellow St. Michael's rain slicker.

"This is Karen's coat," she announced. "I packed it away. You can see how much smaller it is than Alice's coat."

Dom tossed the coat aside. "Means nothing. It was dark down there, remember. She was so frightened, she didn't recognize me. For Christ's sake, Kay, Annie didn't recognize you in broad daylight!"

"I don't know. It doesn't make sense."

"What do you mean it doesn't make sense?" Dom pounded an exasperated fist into his palm. "Everybody's saying your daughter is a killer. Does that make sense?"

Catherine realized he was right, but before she could tell him the phone rang.

"Hello?"

The silence on the other end was both ominous and mocking.

"Hello!" she repeated sharply. When there was no answer, she slammed the receiver down.

"That's been happening since yesterday," Catherine fumed. "I think it was Annie. What does she expect me to do? Call *her* and forgive her?"

Dom's eyes narrowed. "What makes you so sure it's her?"

"Last night Jim was here. The poor fool told me she keeps dialing and hanging up." Catherine shook her head in disgust. "My sister can't stand to be ignored."

"Maybe you should talk to her."

The quiet suggestion fueled her indignation.

"I will . . . *after* she admits she lied about Alice."

"Don't be too hasty. It could be to our advantage. Maybe you'll find out something."

The sound of the phone startled Catherine.

As it continued, Dom smiled encouragingly, but the tension tightened around her body like a wire.

"I can't," she whispered. "I can't do it."

Dom picked up the receiver and extended it toward her. "Try . . . for Alice."

Her hand trembling, Catherine took the phone. "Hello?"

The silence licked obscenely at her ear.

"Hello, Annie? Is that you?" she mumbled. "Talk to me. What do you—"

Unable to go on, Catherine thrust the phone back into Dom's hands. "It's no use. I can't do it. There's too much hate inside."

"Hello, Anna?" Dom said quickly. There was a click as the line disconnected.

Then he heard Catherine's muffled sobbing. She was curled on the sofa, her face pressed against the pillows.

Dom eased beside her, but at his touch, her body clenched like a steel fist.

"It's okay," he whispered, caressing her rigid neck. "I shouldn't have asked you to do it. We'll do it without her. I promise."

As her tension slowly released, Dom drew her close, rocking her gently until the ragged sobs faded into his soothing murmur. "It's going to be okay now. Don't worry. I won't leave you alone again."

She looked up, eyes wide and vulnerable.

His fingers brushed her cheek and traced the smooth contours of her face as if seeing its fragile beauty for the first time.

Catherine touched his hand uncertainly.

"It's all right," he whispered, kissing her fingers. "I'll make everything all right."

"Can you?" she asked, eyes suddenly illuminated. "Can you really?"

She responded eagerly when he kissed her, moaning softly as his hands caressed her breasts. Her husky moans of pleasure deepened and her body pumped insistently against him, moving with an urgency he'd never sensed before.

When the phone rang, she flinched. At the second ring, she moved to answer.

"Don't bother. It's not important," Dom whispered.

"Let me."

"Come back here. Let it ring."

Catherine's smile was fired with determination. "I want to answer. I'm not afraid anymore." She lifted the receiver.

"Annie?"

The confidence illuminating her face went dim. "Yes, he's here. Just a moment."

She held the phone out stiffly. "It's for you."

When Dom heard his wife's voice, he understood Catherine's reaction. His own was equally uncertain.

"Julie? Is something wrong?"

"I didn't mean to bother you, dear. Is it all right?"

Something in Julia's voice alerted him.

"Silly question. Of course it is," he said calmly. "Anything wrong there?"

"Doctor says mother and baby are doing fine."

Guilt and confusion tumbled through his mind. "You mean you had—"

"No, silly, not yet. We have a little time. It's just that I'm kind of lonely and Ginny's here and . . ."

His confusion fled, but the guilt began to take

root. "Look, I'm in the middle of a—legal matter so I can't talk to you right now. I'll call you back."

"I just called to tell you—Ginny insists I stay with them. I keep telling her I'm fine, but it's getting kind of close—and well, they want me there."

"That's a good idea."

Julia seemed disappointed. "I just didn't want you to worry. I mean, if you called and I didn't answer. I'll be there until you come home."

Dom caught the hint. Julia had probably been calling the hotel all day.

"All right, fine," he said, his voice walking a tightrope between neutrality and affection.

"Okay, then. I miss you." Her voice lowered. "Can't wait till you get back. I love you."

"Me too. Take care."

"Me too *what?*" Julia demanded coyly.

Aware of Catherine's intent gaze, Dom half-turned. "I love you," he murmured.

As he put the receiver down, Dom knew that the new sensuality he'd discovered in Catherine was also disconnected. At least for tonight.

"Alice is right," Catherine snapped. "Don't play detective—go home."

"Look, Kay, we're grown-ups now. Did it ever occur to you that home is here, too? Despite what the Vatican says."

"Just because you want to play father doesn't mean you're entitled to play husband."

The righteous edge in her voice signaled an old warning. Dom silently walked to the hall and opened the closet.

Catherine drifted after him, watching as he buttoned his coat.

He looked up. "Just for the record, Catherine . . . I really meant it."

"It doesn't matter."

Something in her curt tone touched a nerve. "Maybe if I were Father Tom . . ." He stopped, but too late. Catherine's face was stony with contempt.

"I'm sorry, Kay," he mumbled. "I don't know why I said that." Then his voice became firmer. "But I am a man, and I can't help being jealous. I always felt if I'd been more like Tom, we'd still be married."

Her expression wavered and she smiled. "Somehow I can't see you as a celibate." Knowing that what he'd said was true, she also understood that her own jealousy had caused her to lash back at Dom. "I'm sorry, too," she said softly. "It would have been good to be held close and pretend it was yesterday."

"Today might be best of all," Dom murmured wistfully. "You're even more beautiful now, you know."

"Now that's very nice." Her smile suddenly broke into a giggle. "We're both so foolish. Even if there was a way of going back, it would start all over again."

"I guess you're right," Dom sighed, coming closer. He kissed her cheek then tenderly leaned his forehead against hers.

"Wonder what the church would say about a ménage à trois."

Catherine swooned back and covered her eyes in mock outrage. "It sounds dirty. You'd better go."

"Pick you up about two tomorrow?"

Her grin faded. "Really, Dom . . . I mean Julia's going to . . . Don't you think you should go back? It's not fair."

"Leave this decision to me," he whispered.

His eyes hovered clear blue and certain above the tight-lipped smile. "I owe this one to Alice."

✠ ✠ ✠

As Dom studied Father Tom's list over breakfast, he felt optimistic.

He'd called home after leaving Catherine's and had a long, loving chat with his wife. Five minutes after hanging up, Julie had called back with an overlooked message from his office.

The message hadn't been important, but Julie's was clear: her unsubtle way of checking that he'd called from the hotel room and not Catherine's apartment.

Knowing Julie felt secure did much to contain the emotions rioting against his efforts to form a logical plan. The phone call to his office this morning quelled them completely.

As of now, his advertising firm was in the process of completing three campaigns and starting another. With luck, his presence wouldn't be required for two months.

Julia's baby wasn't due for six weeks which meant he could stay in Paterson for another month, fly back to Colorado when Julia's time neared, then return to Paterson for at least another month to follow up the investigation.

Dom was a realist and his faith in logic led to his rejection of Catholicism, and ultimately, the divorce. And now more than ever, he reminded himself, was the time to proceed on fact-by-fact logic.

The police were incompetent and the county psychiatrist was worse, but perhaps he could turn that to advantage. He had two months to personally follow up every lead or possibility available. After that he'd know the territory well enough to keep a tight check on any private investigator he hired.

Hopefully he'd come up with proof of Alice's innocence before that. If not the real killer, some piece of evidence like the knife or the missing crucifix.

And the first step was interviewing everyone who owned a St. Michael's raincoat.

Dom ordered a second pot of coffee from room service, then hauled out the telephone directory and started writing numbers. There were less than seven hundred names on the list. At the rate of twenty or so per day, he could cover them in less than a month.

When the phone rang, he thought it was room service calling back.

"Uncle Dom?"

His instincts bristled. "Who's this?"

"Angela." The voice was muffled and indistinct.

"Is something wrong?" Dom asked mildly, despite his rising pulse rate.

"I ran away. I'm hiding. I've got Karen's cross."

The last two words tumbled into his brain like live grenades. Dom smothered them with his will, forcing himself to remain calm.

"Talk louder, I can't hear you."

"I've got Karen's cross and Mommy won't let me give it to you," she sniffled.

"Listen, honey, let me meet you. We can talk about it. Where are you?"

"You'll tell . . ."

"You know better than that," Dom said soothingly. "Has Uncle Dom ever done anything to hurt you? I'll come alone. Promise."

His heartbeat flooded the pause as she considered. "I'm at—I'm near the Ivanhoe Factory on River Street," she blurted then began crying again.

"Easy now, honey, I'll be there in fifteen minutes," Dom said gently, will still wrapped around his excitement.

When she hung up, the grenades exploded, demolishing all doubt. He'd been right about Angela. It all made sense now.

Especially Annie's determination to blame Alice. The bitch wanted to shield her own daughter. She wanted to sacrifice little Alice for a crime she'd never committed. Her own sister's child.

But that cross would expose the truth, Dom exulted, sweeping up the car keys.

By the time room service arrived with his coffee, he was rolling out of the parking lot.

✠ ✠ ✠

Abandoned factories lined both sides of River Street, looming above the low tenements like tombstones over wooden graves. Dom had trouble locating the building Angela had mentioned and finally stopped at a candy store for directions.

The Ivanhoe Factory was a squat four-story building surrounded by a wire fence. The faded sign above the gate read: IVANHOE LOCOMOTIVE. The gate was locked.

There was a phone booth on the corner, but Angela wasn't there.

Dom returned to the factory and walked slowly along the fence until he spotted a ragged opening. The hole was narrow, but he managed to squeeze through. Once inside, he approached the building slowly.

All the windows were smashed and a side door had been pulled from its hinges, giving him many routes to choose from. The question: which one—if any—would lead him to Angela. The place looked deserted. It could be some sort of weird prank.

"Hsst."

His eyes groped toward the sound and saw the small figure in the yellow hooded raincoat, standing at the side door.

"Angela?"

She ducked back inside as he moved closer.

"Angela, it's me," Dom called, but when he reached the doorway, it was empty. He stood a moment letting his vision adjust to the dim light before walking slowly to the concrete stairway.

He had to take his time, gain her confidence, Dom thought, peering up at the shadows.

There was a faint crunching noise above him, like glass being crushed under someone's heel.

"Angela? Don't you want to talk?" he called.

His question echoed through the quiet gloom.

Dom was careful to keep his voice steady as he climbed the stairway.

"Be careful, it's dangerous here. You might get cut on this broken glass."

The only response was the sound of his own patient footsteps on the stairs.

When they hit the second landing, she popped out, a smiling jack-in-the-box, with a clown face and a heavy steel knife that jolted surprise into his flesh like an electric buzzer. Dom's brain didn't register the shock until he saw the blade coiling back, its red tip angled for his throat.

Reflex swept his arm across his neck and he grabbed her wrist, twisting it back.

"Jesus Christ! What are you doing?" he shouted.

Dom's belly seemed to burst open when her knee rammed into his groin. The agony toppled his balance, but he desperately held her wrist, pulling her with him.

As she jerked free, the knife jumped out of her fingers and clattered to the bottom of the stairway.

Dom looked up, rage filtering through his pain.

"You little bitch, wait till I get hold of you, Angela," he groaned, lurching toward the masked girl poised above him.

Still crippled by the kick, he wasn't nearly fast enough. She scampered up the stairs and ducked out of sight on the next landing.

Rage kept Dom moving despite the spasms in his groin. He approached the next landing with extreme caution, then saw the entrance was boarded shut.

He ducked at a sudden flutter of sound above him. Two pigeons flew into the hall and dove through a window.

Dom took two stairs at a time as the spasms ebbed and the anger expanded.

"It's no use," he yelled. "I'm going to get you, Angela."

The entrance to the top floor was open, and Dom stood in the doorway scanning an immense loft the size of a football field. Two lines of concrete pillars formed a huge aisle to the large loading doors at the other end of the loft.

A patch of yellow raincoat was protruding from behind one of the columns nearby.

Suddenly aware of an oily warmth, Dom looked down and saw that his hand was covered by a glistening red glove. The sight of the blood somehow cooled his anger.

The wound on his arm began throbbing as he walked slowly to the girl hiding behind the concrete pillar.

She kept her back turned, body tensed for flight.

"Don't run, Angela. I'm not mad at you anymore," he said softly. "I want to help you. You don't have to be afraid of me. I'll . . ."

The pink face grinned merrily when she whirled, as if the object hefted in her hand was a pie instead of the brick that slammed him unconscious.

✣ ✣ ✣

The figure stood uncertainly above Dom's inert body. The brick cracked in half on the impact, but he was still breathing, she speculated. If she went back for the knife, he might wake up.

She rummaged through the debris in the loft but found nothing heavy enough to kill him—not even another brick.

She saw a length of heavy rope dangling beside a window. She hurried to the window and yanked the rope loose, realizing she could keep him tied while she went down for the knife.

But as she webbed the rope around Dom's body, the masked figure noticed the loading doors at the end of the loft.

After knotting the rope securely, she hurried to the doors and pulled them back, flooding the room with sunlight.

Then she went back to Dom and started rolling his trussed body to the platform.

It proved to be slow, tiring work, and in a few minutes the small, masked figure was gasping heavily. She tried moving the heavy body by lifting first the shoulders, then the feet; but that was also too strenuous.

When Dom regained consciousness, the girl was sitting on the floor, methodically kicking him toward the open door.

Dazed at first, he didn't understand what she was doing, but the pain shooting into his side forced his blurred thoughts into focus. As he blinked at the light spilling through the open door, the horror of what she intended seeped into his brain like acid.

Desperately he twisted against the ropes. "Angela! Don't do this to me!" he yelled.

The girl remained intent on her task. Weary of kicking him, she resumed rolling his bundled weight to the doorway.

"Help!" Dom roared, as he saw the edge of the platform come closer. "Help me!"

He lifted his head toward Angela. "You can't do this. God will punish you."

She stopped pushing and peered down at him. As she leaned closer, Dom saw the antique gold crucifix dangling from her neck and realized that it must be Karen's cross.

"I knew you wouldn't," Dom said, voice trembling and husky. "Now untie me and . . ."

"Filthy pig. You and that whore—*that's* who God wants punished."

Dom's eyes widened at the deep, vaguely familiar voice, and then bulged in numbed shock as the woman ripped the mask from her face.

"Father Tom belongs to the church," she rasped. "I am his protector."

"Holy Christ . . ." Dom stammered, writhing and thrashing against the bonds. "Mrs. Tredoni! Mrs. Tredoni! . . . my God . . . why?"

Her raincoat fell open, revealing the white communion dress as she bobbed over him like a rabid, panting dog, lips curled back from her sharp teeth.

"St. Michael the Archangel defend us in battle . . ." she intoned as she pushed him toward the edge of the loading platform.

"Mrs. Tredoni, don't do this!" Dom pleaded.

". . . be our protection against the snares of the devil . . ."

In a frantic effort to stop her, Dom lunged savagely, trying to bite her throat. His animallike snap missed her neck but caught Karen's cross. Teeth clenched, he jerked back, breaking the thin gold chain.

Mrs. Tredoni stopped and tried to pull the crucifix loose. "Give me that!" she rasped. "It's mine!"

Sensing that the cross could be his salvation,

Dom sucked it into his mouth and clamped his jaws.

Mrs. Tredoni clawed at his mouth, raking vivid red streaks across his face with her nails, fingers digging for leverage as she tried to pry his jaw open.

Dom jerked and twisted constantly, making it impossible.

In a sudden fit of hysterical frenzy, she tore off her shoe and wildly smacked at his mouth.

"Pig . . . it's mine . . . give it to me!"

Dom's lips became a gurgling smear of pulped flesh, but he refused to release the cross.

Infuriated, Mrs. Tredoni kicked him toward the open door, continuing her prayer in a hoarse, labored whisper.

"We humbly beseech God to command him. Do thou oh prince of the heavenly host . . . by the divine power . . ."

"You're going . . . to get caught."

Dom almost choked on the cross but kept it behind his clenched teeth. "Tom . . . will find you out . . ." he groaned, eyes fixed on the dazzling emptiness looming closer.

". . . thrust into hell Satan and the other evil spirits who roam the world seeking the ruin of souls . . ."

The blazing sun spun madly through his screaming brain, then collided with total darkness.

10

The woman knelt in the last row of pews, head bowed, breath scratching rapidly against the silence.

Suddenly the altar erupted with light.

The woman stiffened, grabbed her shopping bag, and left the pew; scuttling back to the shadows like a yellow roach.

She froze when she heard the footsteps trooping across the lobby.

Back pressed against the wall, she moved swiftly toward the storeroom. Realizing there wasn't time, she scurried into the confessional booth as the children entered the church.

Sweating heavily, Mrs. Tredoni sat on the small bench and pulled off her raincoat. Her loud gasps filled the booth as she unbuttoned the white dress. They stopped as the murmur outside quieted.

"All right, now. Let's get settled quickly. We don't want to keep Father Tom waiting."

Mrs. Tredoni held her breath and peered through the slit in the curtain.

The last rows nearest the confessional were occupied by children. They remained somber under Sister Felicia's stern eye, but brightened visibly when Father Tom approached.

"Hello, Father Tom," they chorused.

Mrs. Tredoni could not quite see his face, but noticed the purple and black strip of fabric he was carrying. It was the penitential stole, she realized with a flutter of panic. He was going to hear confession. She had to hurry.

She reached into the shopping bag for her housedress and black oxfords. She had to change the shoes first; there was blood on them.

She slipped off the white communion shoes as Father Tom addressed the children.

"This will be your last confession as a group. Think carefully about what you want to say. But remember; I don't have to hear *everything* you've done since Sunday. After all, we don't want Sister Felicia to miss her lunch."

The children began giggling.

"Settle down," Sister Felicia admonished crisply. "Everybody ready? Let's make a good Act of Contrition."

As the young voices began chanting the traditional prayer, Mrs. Tredoni jammed the folded raincoat into the bag, covering the shoes and knife. The white dress went on top of the raincoat to protect it from bloodstains. She was struggling into the housedress when Father Tom entered the center stall and slid open the grated panel separating priest from penitent.

He was surprised to see a silhouetted profile through the screen.

"Someone in here?"

Mrs. Tredoni fell to her knees.

"Bless me, Father, for I have sinned . . ." she whispered hurriedly.

"We're hearing only the children this morning," Father Tom said.

"Bless me, Father, for I have sinned . . ." she insisted, screwing one shoe over her foot.

"Mrs. Tredoni, is that you? What's wrong?"

She reached for the other shoe. "Please hear me, Father. I'm troubled."

"Go ahead. I have time," he assured.

Mrs. Tredoni raked her brain for something to tell him as she slipped her toe into the oxford.

"I lost my temper with Father Pat . . . and I neglected my morning prayers. . . ."

"This can't be the reason you wanted confession this morning," he prompted mildly.

"Oh, no, Father, there is something . . ." she mumbled, unable to squeeze her foot into the oxford.

"Yes . . . ?" Receiving no reply, Tom coaxed her gently. "I know you, Mrs. Tredoni. . . . You're a good woman. . . . It can't be as bad as you think."

"I'm losing patience with the monsignor," she blurted, jerking the shoe over her foot. "Oh, Father, I remember when everyone respected him so."

"I understand. It's not easy to see someone we love suffer."

"You don't understand. Sometimes I think it would be better if . . . but it's a sin to have such thoughts."

"It's not a sin. You've devoted so much of yourself to us that it's only natural that you would want God to spare us from the pain."

Mrs. Tredoni's hands paused at the buttons of her housedress. She leaned against the partition, exhaustion and panic miraculously dispelled by

Father Tom's words. Truly he was a saint, she exulted.

"You have great faith. It's because of this that you can look to death as a resolution. There is no greater reward than to spend eternity with our Lord."

She knew it was a sign from St. Michael.

He was speaking through Father Tom to bless her holy mission. "Oh, yes, Father," Mrs. Tredoni said joyously.

As she started buttoning the dress, her fingers brushed her breast. The contact stiffened her nipples with a sudden spark of sensation that ignited her senses.

"I'm sorry you didn't come to me sooner," Father Tom said.

"I am, too," she whispered, hand sliding down her sweat-greased skin to the matted patch of hair at the edge of her belly.

"There's no need to go to confession for this. When you're upset, come to me. I'm your confessor, but I'm also your friend."

Listening to his vibrant voice she understood she was the bride of Christ in his body and blood. Her soul was illuminated by a burst of holy light as her fingers stoked the inferno steaming her flesh.

"Oh, thank you, Father!" she exclaimed.

Mrs. Tredoni was still rapt in exultation when she left the booth. She strode proudly to the altar, oblivious of the waiting line of children who stared at her in hushed fascination as she passed.

✠ ✠ ✠

Dr. Profano went about his work with weary detachment. After ten years as the county medical examiner, death held few surprises.

"There is a ten-centimeter laceration of the dorsum of the left forearm," he droned to the assistant scribbling notes.

He dropped the arm and circled the metal table. "Right humerus is fractured. Contusions and abrasions of the thorax. Right clavicle is fractured." Dr. Profano moved Dominic Spages's head from side to side. "It appears that the cervical spine is fractured. Please note hematomas of the lips," he added, inserting his finger into the ruined mouth.

He touched something odd. Squinting, he bent closer and saw the gold chain clenched between the teeth. When tugging didn't dislodge it, he extended an upraised palm toward his assistant. "Pass me the laryngoscope."

Pleased by his assistant's crisp operating-room response, Dr. Profano used the instrument to force the clamped jaws open and illuminate the throat. Then he fished up the chain with a forceps.

As the chain emerged, the antique gold crucifix gleamed in the light of the laryngoscope.

"Now, that's what I call taking your religion seriously," he observed, dropping the cross into a tin pan.

The assistant looked down nervously, upset more by the remark than by the object he'd discovered in Dominic Spages's throat.

It was the first personal comment Dr. Profano had ever made about a patient.

✠ ✠ ✠

As he waited for the results of the autopsy, Father Tom knew that he'd failed his friend. Much of what happened was directly his fault. And it began long before Dom's death.

He'd taken Catherine's part during the breakup

of their marriage, telling himself it was for the sake of morality, church law, and his concern for the children. But he knew better now. Dom's death hammered the reality into his brain.

He'd harbored a personal jealousy of Dom's ability to break free and forge a life on his own terms.

Behind the piety and the prayer he was just another hypocrite, Father Tom reflected bitterly.

He'd always been envious of Dom in high school because of Catherine. And even now, after his vows and years of celibacy, he felt that same attraction to her.

Perhaps it was that attraction that caused him to set up barriers between Catherine and Dom. Perhaps it was the reason for his resistance to Dom's investigation of Karen's murder—and his eagerness to blame Alice. Certainly he couldn't deny the carnal yearning he felt for Catherine any longer. Not now, when his friend had given his life for the truth.

Father Tom paced silently, hands stuffed into his pockets, then moved to the phone booth. His sins weren't important at the moment, he reminded, groping for a coin. Catherine needed his unselfish support.

"She's not at the rectory," he announced, hanging up the phone. "And she's not home. I'm getting worried."

Captain Beame's doughy face remained hopeful when he looked up from his magazine.

"I'm sure nothing's happened to her, Father Tom."

"If the shelter says she left at two-thirty, she should be home by now," Detective Spina said.

Beame shot him an annoyed glance. "Close that door."

He noted Spina's wordless obedience with satisfaction. In the last few hours, his partner had ceased to be a problem.

"Damn it, why did he go down there?" Father Tom railed helplessly.

"Did he give you any indication that he knew something?"

"Last time I saw him, I gave him a list of families who bought those school coats. He was convinced that Alice had confused Karen with someone else." He paused, then decided to tell it all. "Because of Annie, he suspected Angela, his niece."

"Can you get me a copy of that list?"

"We never did find out where that kid was," Spina put in.

Beame's flare of anger was defused when the doctor emerged from the examination room and hurried toward him.

"You're not going to believe this," Profano drawled, unfolding a swatch of muslin. "It was lodged in his throat."

Father Tom gaped disbelievingly at the glimmering object. "It's Karen's cross."

"It had to be worn by the killer," Dr. Profano observed cheerfully. "It wasn't forced down his throat. He bit down on it. Look at the teeth marks."

Captain Beame examined the crucifix closely. "Is this all there was of the chain?"

"We're checking the contents of his stomach now."

"This accounts for the bruises on his mouth," Beame mused.

Dr. Profano nodded emphatic agreement. "Whoever killed him wanted that cross very badly."

The remark bit into Father Tom's emotions like a drill. His mother's crucifix had become a hellish pawn through his own weakness, but he wouldn't allow Dom's death to be wasted.

Spina snapped his fingers. "I better have someone check where that kid was today."

The captain's scowl cooled his enthusiasm. "Before you take care of that important detail," Beame said caustically, "maybe you can find time to order a release on Alice Spages."

Spina winced and hurried to comply.

"Father, do you have a number where we can reach his family?"

"There's just his wife. Let me make the call. I think it would be better if I tell her brother and let him break it to her."

Father Tom stared down at the cross, his voice barely audible. "She's pregnant."

✣ ✣ ✣

The doorbell interrupted Mrs. Tredoni's dinner preparations. Exasperated, she put the carving knife aside and left the kitchen to answer. When she saw Catherine Spages at the door, her annoyance escalated sharply.

"I'm sorry to bother you" she said sweetly.

Mrs. Tredoni wasn't fooled. "Father Tom's not here."

"I'm looking for Mr. Spages. I know he had to drop off Father Tom's car."

Despite a flutter of panic, Mrs. Tredoni's face remained impassive. "I haven't seen him. You'll have to excuse me, I'm preparing supper."

"Do you mind if I wait?" she pressed. "Maybe they're together. I'm a little concerned."

"Suit yourself," Mrs. Tredoni said, stepping back from the door. "But he may be gone for some time."

"I'm sure they're together," Catherine repeated lamely. "Do you think there's something wrong with the phone? I called several times, but there was no answer."

"I was out," the housekeeper snapped.

"Well . . . of course . . ."

Catherine's surprised expression warned Mrs. Tredoni to control her hostility. It would only arouse suspicion. *Much better to show a smiling face,* she thought. *Like the mask.*

"I have some coffee made," she said genially. "It's in the kitchen. Come—you can wait with me there while I work."

Catherine accepted gratefully, but as she followed the tiny housekeeper, was uncomfortably aware of a sense of intrusion.

It increased when she entered the kitchen.

Its impeccable neatness was ominous somehow, like the forbidding precision of an operating room. Mrs. Tredoni's curt manner made her discomfort complete.

"Sit down," she ordered.

Catherine sat at the table and watched the small hawk-faced housekeeper move about the kitchen with grim efficiency.

"This is very nice of you," she smiled, trying to be positive.

Mrs. Tredoni poured her a cup of coffee, then returned the pot to the stove.

"Aren't you having any?" Catherine asked politely.

"I make it a rule never to have coffee after breakfast."

The disclosure seemed to discourage further conversation. Catherine drank her coffee, the silence becoming more oppressive with each sip.

Mrs. Tredoni was also disturbed. Although determined to appear hospitable, her passions were surging violently against her control. She deeply regretted bringing her into the kitchen. The woman's presence defiled the sanctity of her private domain.

Emotions mounting, she took a brown paper bag from the refrigerator and dropped it on the table on the way to the cutlery drawer.

She returned with a heavy carving knife, slit the bag open, and unwrapped a large fish.

"I guess this is really silly of me," Catherine murmured. "I really should go home. I don't know why I get so worried. It's just that I don't know where he could be."

The fish's eyes regarded Mrs. Tredoni with astonishment as she deftly severed its head.

"Maybe you're afraid God will send St. Michael to take another of your loved ones."

The statement caught Catherine off guard. Unnerved and anxious to leave, she watched the fierce little woman scale the fish.

"When St. Michael took my little girl, I thought only how cruel God was," Mrs. Tredoni muttered, half to herself.

Catherine's eyes widened. "I'm sorry, Mrs. Tredoni. I never knew you had a little girl."

"Don't you see? He wanted to teach me." She gestured with the knife and moved closer. "We pay for the sins of our parents. I was sent here to take care of Father Tom."

Catherine nodded, eyes frozen on the knife jabbing nearer like an indignant finger.

"Mrs. Tredoni!" Father Tom's voice broke the spell.

Catherine stood up quickly. "It's Tom!" she exclaimed, her voice breathless with relief.

She hurried out of the kitchen to the entrance hall.

The blood pounded hotly against Mrs. Tredoni's temples as she watched the woman leave. Her hate was too strong to suppress; another moment, and she'd have executed the whore right there. Only the intervention of St. Michael prevented a serious blunder.

She moved to the door and listened.

"Tom . . . I've been . . ."

"Catherine, what are you doing here? I've been looking for you all afternoon."

"Where's Dom? Is something wrong?"

"There's been an accident."

"Dominic!" Catherine screamed. "Oh, Tom . . . Tom, please . . . help me . . ." Father Tom embraced Catherine, trying to calm her down.

Mrs. Tredoni shut the door on Catherine's wailing, knowing it was just the harlot's way of tempting Father Tom closer.

But soon the devil's mistress would know the vengeance of St. Michael, she reflected, her hand stroking her throat as it groped for the missing cross.

✠ ✠ ✠

Father Tom watched his life parade before him as Dom's casket was being wheeled to the plane.

In the past twenty hours, he'd questioned every belief that glued his soul together—including his faith in God—and found no answers.

All he'd discovered was that he'd yet to be tested as a man. For years he'd been protected; first by his mother, and then by the church. Almost half his life was gone, and he was just as dead as his friend.

At least Dom had partaken of the feast while he was young and alive.

If God existed, then he'd been a useless servant to the Lord, Father Tom decided. He gave nothing to the Lord's house and used nothing of its bounty. It took Dom's death to show him the meaning of a true vocation.

If he really intended to serve God, he would serve as a man—not a symbol. In a few weeks he'd go into retreat and decide if he wished to remain a priest.

Catherine, too, was pondering lost chances and a new life while watching Dom's casket being loaded onto the plane.

Dom had tried to show her so many things, but

she'd been blinded by stubborn pride. Instead of accepting the man who was real, she'd rejected human love for a series of childish fairy tales. Dom had been right about Father Tom. Her admiration for the priest—perhaps even her devoutness—were safe ways of preserving her virginal fantasy.

She'd lost too much to keep that image intact. Maybe there'd never be another chance for a new start, but she wouldn't return to a dream lover. She couldn't let Alice be sacrificed for her failures.

She'd learn to accept all of life, if only to save her daughter.

But Catherine's awakening didn't quell the yawning terror at the core of her awareness.

Someone wanted to kill her family, and she didn't know why.

Catherine and Father Tom waited until the cargo door closed, then walked slowly back to the limousine, oblivious to the gusting sheets of rain that whipped across the open field.

As the limousine pulled away, Catherine looked back through the water-streaked window at the plane lifting off the runway.

"I'm not going to tell her just yet," Catherine said softly. "She's been without a father for a long time. I'm not going to take him away from her so soon."

She fingered the antique cross around her neck. "I understand what he meant now—about being torn between two worlds. A part of me has gone with him."

Emotions riddled Father Tom's thoughts like machine-gun bullets.

He was tempted to tell Catherine about his decision—then realized it would confuse, rather than comfort her. It wasn't the moment for plans but for strength. He had to help Catherine and Alice find each other before he could search out his own salvation.

If he found it, there might be a time for them someday.

Catherine gazed at the monotonous blur of apartment buildings that edged the highway. There was something invulnerable about the faceless dwellings; as if their sameness shielded their inhabitants from tragedy.

"I can't live with this feeling," she said suddenly. "Why have I lost control of my life?"

Tom leaned closer. "You haven't lost control. Death does this to people."

"Haven't I had more than my share?"

"There is no such thing as a share," he said softly.

For a long time she was silent, brooding to the rhythmic hiss of rain against the roof. But when the limousine crawled past the gates of the Sarah Reed Children's Center, Catherine's agitation flared.

"Tom, I'm frightened. Maybe I should leave her here. At least here she's safe."

"Don't be ridiculous, Kay. She needs you now." He lowered his voice, knowing that for Alice's sake he had to convince her.

"The child has been through enough hell. I promise you there's nothing to fear."

Catherine's blood froze at the promise, remembering what Dom had said the night before he was killed.

"For how long are any of us safe, Tom? What happens if they don't find the murderer?"

The steely edge in her question shredded all his convictions except one.

"Alice is waiting," he reminded.

She was sitting inside the living room when they arrived, coat buttoned and suitcase packed. Her face flooded with glee when the matron unlocked the door, and she eagerly jumped to her feet.

"I'm all ready," Alice announced. Then she hesitated, the eagerness trickling away as she looked from her mother to the priest.

"Where's Daddy?"

Catherine forced a smile. "He had to go back."

"How come?" Alice demanded.

"Let's go home. We'll talk about it later."

Catherine picked up the suitcase, but Alice refused to move. She glared at her mother, stubby features locked in sullen resentment.

"He didn't even say good-bye," she said contemptuously.

Catherine dropped the suitcase and knelt beside her. "Please don't feel that way. He kept his promise to you—remember that."

She gripped her daughter's shoulders tightly, her voice wavering as she fought back the tears.

"It's because of him that you're coming home," she whispered. "Never forget that."

Alice didn't answer, hypnotized by the heavy gold crucifix that dangled from her mother's neck.

✠ ✠ ✠

Mrs. Tredoni placed the knife and the yellow raincoat inside her shopping bag, then slowly walked across the room.

There was no need to hurry because St. Michael had appeared to her and given his miraculous blessing.

She could not fail; today she would slay the whore of Babylon.

Dressed in her white communion dress, white shoes and lace gloves, Mrs. Tredoni paused to examine the collection of dolls arranged around her small bedroom. She favored each with her special attention.

The dolls were more than mere ornaments. On

those nights when the Holy Ghost filled the room with sanctifying grace, the dolls would come alive. They laughed and danced and chattered wonderful secrets.

But today they were silent, awed by the magnificent apparition of St. Michael. He'd come to her again, just the way he came the night her own Michela was entombed.

Mrs. Tredoni understood why her lovely daughter had been taken. Her own heinous sins had been responsible for the child's death. But she'd been granted a divine boon of redemption through the intercession of the holy saint.

St. Michael had come down in a mantle of white flame and revealed her destiny. She'd been chosen to wield his sword on earth. Chosen to strike down the evil ones who sought to prevent Father Tom from fulfilling his divine mission.

Mrs. Tredoni moved to the large plaster statue of St. Michael on the bureau and looked at the photographs propped up beside him. There was one of a tall, exceptionally handsome man, in a dark suit; another of a young girl with wide, pretty eyes; the third was of Father Tom.

Even when she gazed closely at the first photograph, it was difficult to see any similarity between the aristocratic figure smiling at her—and the ruined husk of the monsignor.

It was her carnal lust for the beautiful young priest in the photograph that marked her daughter's fate. Lust that branded Michela for sacrifice even as she flowered in her mother's womb.

Mrs. Tredoni was an innocent student from a good family in Palermo when World War II erupted. Five horrendous years later, her family had been slaughtered and she'd been raped by soldiers of both the German and the American armies.

She'd come to America as a refugee and was

taken in by the Sisters of Mercy. She'd learned quickly and soon found work at St. Michael's Rectory.

The first pastor had been an elderly scholar, and from him she'd learned to love books and music.

He left after two years to pursue his studies at the Vatican Library and a new priest was assigned to the parish.

Father Giovani was handsome, well bred, and ambitious. He'd taught her the ceremonies of church politics, and the art of sensuality.

The rectory was a salon for the rich and talented, and Father Giovani was an inspired host. He courted power as if it were an empress and cultivated pleasure as if he was beyond sin.

He'd seduced her one hot, sultry afternoon. Afterward, when the enormity of her crime sent her into a weeping frenzy, he solemnly donned his penitential stole and gave her absolution.

From that day she was his secretary, confidante, and mistress. He schooled her in the rituals of human lust, and she fell in love for the first and only time.

In a short while the aristocratic priest was made monsignor, and many predicted he'd become the youngest bishop in America.

It was the happiest period of her life. He needed her then and together they forged the new links of his ambitions. The modest parish became endowed with the splendor of a Renaissance court, and she was privileged far beyond her rank as rectory housekeeper.

When she discovered she was pregnant, the entire matter was settled in hours. She was provided with a marriage certificate to one Ralph Tredoni and a train ticket to Washington, D.C.

She'd rented an apartment, and the monsignor would visit on alternate weekends, always with a gift and an envelope full of cash. It was during those serene months that he'd started giving her the dolls.

Two months after she gave birth to Michela, the monsignor procured a death certificate for the fictitious Ralph Tredoni, and she returned to the rectory as a widowed housekeeper with a new name and an infant daughter.

The years settled into contentment. Michela enjoyed her mother's love and her father's devotion. All three shared a rare gift.

The monsignor wanted more, however.

He became arrogant, casting all semblance of priestly duties aside in pursuit of his vain ambitions. His contant striving gained him many choice diplomatic assignments. He was away for months at a time, but news of his success reached as far as the humble rectory.

Mrs. Tredoni knew then there were other women, but it didn't seem important, as long as he was fulfilling his destiny. She understood his beauty was a special grace from God.

But he fell from grace abruptly, when Michela was eight years old. That very month, while he was at a convocation in Paris, the vacant bishopric in Paterson was given to a local monsignor.

While Monsignor Giovani had been seeking honor, the faithful parishioners in his care had been left woefully unattended, and the oversight had offended too many former supporters.

The monsignor returned to St. Michael's an embittered, pompous glutton. His thirsts for alcohol and young women were his only interests.

Even Michela ceased to mean anything to him.

But Mrs. Tredoni continued to love him, hoping that he'd be inspired by the divine spirit and regain his faith.

She perservered, giving Michela all the devotion she needed to become a lovely young lady.

As the time for Michela's First Communion neared, Mrs. Tredoni's hopes for the monsignor intensified.

She believed passionately that when he celebrated that mass and gave the Holy Sacrament to his daughter, the sanctifying grace would touch his soul.

She hadn't reckoned on the price for her own wanton crime.

The day before her daughter's First Communion, Michela complained of a headache and went to bed with a high fever. Six hours later, she was dead.

The doctors had discovered a blood clot on her brain but Mrs. Tredoni knew they were wrong. St. Michael himself appeared in his miraculous glory to tell her the truth.

She and her monsignor had defied God with their lust and brazen lies.

But she'd been given an opportunity for atonement, Mrs. Tredoni reflected gratefully. That very week, she'd executed the first one. A young slut who was the monsignor's current pet.

There were others, until the monsignor's stroke curtailed his lechery and Father Tom was appointed pastor.

The young priest was like a vessel of divine fire that cleansed the rectory of corruption. Father Tom restored the living Spirit of Christ to the entire parish.

The monsignor was left to bear the agony of his sins, but she'd been given the chance for restitution.

She would make certain that the temporal lusts of Satan didn't snare Father Tom the way it had her beautiful monsignor.

Mrs. Tredoni made the sign of the cross, then touched St. Michael's plaster foot. She let her hand linger on the statue, drawing the purifying energy into her body before she reached down and pulled open the bottom drawer of her dresser.

Digging beneath her rolled cotton underwear, she removed the white veil and the mask.

It was Michela's communion veil. The veil she never wore. And her very special talisman.

With her veil and sword, she'd defend God's son on earth from the temptations of the wicked. Temptations like that slut who coiled around his heart like a brightly colored snake.

The bitch Karen had paid for her transgressions, and today her mother would be judged.

Mrs. Tredoni beamed affectionately at the mask. "You're so pretty," she chirped. "Just like my Michela." She kissed the cupid lips then tucked the mask over the knife in the shopping bag.

✠ ✠ ✠

Alice waited patiently for her mother to finish dressing. She stood obediently near the door, in her raincoat, until she remembered something.

She opened the door and peered down the stairs, wondering if she had enough time.

"Don't leave the apartment," Catherine called. "I'll be ready in five minutes. I want to leave early."

Alice slipped out and hurried down the stairs. Five minutes was plenty for what she had in mind.

Less than four minutes later, she returned from the basement and climbed quickly to Alphonso's apartment, her hand covering a bulge in her pocket.

She stood outside the door listening for a moment. Then she recognized the strangled wheeze of his snoring and turned the knob.

As usual, it was unlocked.

And as usual on Sunday mornings, Alphonso was on the couch, dead drunk.

His massive folds of flab spilled over the sides of the couch, shuddering with each slack-jawed rasp. There was an empty gin bottle on the floor, just beneath his grimy fingers.

Her breath held against the stench of urine, sweat, and decayed food, Alice moved inside, picking her way carefully through the debris.

The cat sleeping on Alphonso's belly woke up as Alice tiptoed toward the couch. Its back arched and eyes narrowed as Alice pulled the glass jar from her coat.

When Alice unscrewed the lid and dumped the roaches over Alphonso's greasy pillow, the cat jumped off the couch and ducked behind a pile of trash.

Alice watched the roaches scurry for cover.

Some crawled beneath Alphonso's damp bathrobe. Others spread across his quivering body and lost themselves in the couch.

Catherine was coming down the stairs as Alice left Alphonso's apartment. Although alarmed by her daughter's disappearance, Catherine was determined not to show it. They somehow had to return to a normal way of life, free of fear.

"What were you doing in there?" she asked casually.

Alice shrugged. "I was just saying hello to Mr. Alphonso."

Catherine beamed and patted her head. "I'm glad you did that. In fact, I'm proud of you."

* * *

Detective Spina was fresh out of cigarettes.

He crushed the empty pack disgustedly, then searched behind the visor for a spare. No such luck, he noted bitterly.

Ever since he'd gone off the deep end with that Alice Spages brat, Beame was pouring it on.

Like this stake-out detail for instance.

Beame ordered him to watch the Spages house until relieved, and then conveniently forgot to assign him a partner. Which meant that anytime he left his station to take a leak, his career was on the line.

If that psycho decided to hit the Spages place while he was on a break, Beame would make it a personal crusade to bust his ass back to patrolman.

Spina sighed dejectedly. He couldn't understand it. He didn't finger the kid—her own aunt did that. But Beame acted like he'd molested the brat.

The son of a bitch was jealous, Spina decided for the fortieth time. He'd just been waiting for something like this.

Spina frisked his pockets as two children left a nearby candy store. He watched them whirling hula hoops around their hips as they skipped away, then turned longingly to the candy store.

Duty wrestled briefly with hunger—and lost.

Spina scanned the street for a minute, then reached down and keyed the mike.

"Detective unit thirty-one to headquarters."

A static-cracked voice responded immediately. "Go ahead thirty-one."

"I'll be Code eleven for five minutes."

"Ten-Four."

Spina left the car and walked quickly to the candy store. Two packs of butts and a coffee to go shouldn't take more than five minutes, with any luck.

There wasn't any at all.

The busty blonde waitress made a mistake with the coffee order and served him a cup instead of a take-out container.

"What the hell, I'll drink it," Spina told her, flashing his heartbreaker grin. "Just make me up another to go."

That was strike two.

During the few extra minutes he lingered in the candy store, he missed Catherine and Alice Spages's exit from the apartment building.

He kept glancing outside, but his view of the street was partially blocked by the display of masks strung across the window.

Strike three came when he failed to see Mrs. Tredoni move along the Spages driveway and enter the basement.

* * *

It took Mrs. Tredoni very little time to change her coat, conceal her shopping bag behind a garbage can, and carefully climb the basement stairway to the hall.

Although the front door was secured by a solid spring lock, the basement door was always left open.

After checking to make sure the stairs were clear, she moved soundlessly to the top floor.

When she reached the Spages apartment, she paused to prepare herself. She adjusted the pink plastic face, gripped the heavy knife tightly, and rapped loudly on the door.

A moment later, someone below began squealing in hysterical terror. "Stop it! Help! Stop it!"

His screams touched off a rapid chain reaction that ignited Mrs. Tredoni's instincts like a fiery pinwheel. Whirling, she dashed down the stairs to the basement. As she swung around the banister, Alphonso exploded from his apartment, frenziedly flapping his robe to dislodge the large roaches inside.

"Stop it . . . get out . . ."

Alphonso spotted the grinning mask and bellowed with rage and fear.

"Alice! You little bitch! I'll teach you . . . I'll . . ."

His hands clawed out and ripped the mask away. The unexpected face stunned Alphonso into gasping silence.

Mrs. Tredoni sprang, knife hooking up into Alphonso's groin. The blade entered with a wet, spongy sound, as if smacking an overripe melon.

Gibbering insanely, Alphonso stared at the gray fat curling back like the lips of an oversized vagina, from the oozing red wound in his belly. Then the knife chopped at him again, and his howling screeches filled the stairwell.

"Oh, God! Help me! Help me!"

Mrs. Tredoni stabbed at him frantically, blade punching into the floundering blob who blocked her escape like some massive jellyfish.

"For God's sake! Help! Somebody help!" he blubbered, oily red geysers spurting from his gashed flesh as Mrs. Tredoni raced downstairs.

His continuous sirenlike screams followed her to the entrance. She flung open the door, saw Spina's fish-eyed gawk, slammed the door in his face, and scrambled to the basement.

Above her, Spina wrapped his coat around his wrist and smashed the glass panel of the front door. He reached inside, twisted the knob, and sprinted toward Alphonso's agonized squalls.

"Shit!" Spina roared, as he leaped up the stairs. "Of all the shitty luck!"

11

The children's mass, held the week after First Communion Sunday, was a popular event in St. Michael's Parish.

A special section in the front was reserved for members of the First Communion class, and the church was always crowded with proud families.

Since Tom had celebrated the First Communion mass, his assistant, Father Pat, was officiating that day.

The altar bells jingled for attention as the balding, rotund priest elevated the Host and then uncovered the chalice to continue the consecration of the wine.

Mrs. Tredoni stood at the rear of the church, her head bowed. At the sound of the bells, she glanced nervously around. When she saw Alice Spages in the pew near the center aisle, she couldn't contain her need. She had to be close to her.

The desire scratched at her senses like a raw, physical hunger. Even though Mrs. Tredoni knew that the consecration was the most solemn part of the mass, she found herself moving toward the child. Then she saw Catherine, and the hunger swarmed over her perceptions like excited bees. The restless humming filled her brain as she neared, the shopping bag clutched in front of her.

Mrs. Tredoni stared fixedly at their backs as she jammed herself into the already crowded pew behind them, disregarding the angry murmurs of the parishioners who were forced to move over.

Mrs. Tredoni couldn't comprehend how she'd failed, after St. Michael's visitation. Why would the holy saint deceive her? Was it still another test? She needed a sign, and was certain the Spages woman would reveal it to her.

Some instinct turned Alice around in her seat. She blinked once when she saw Mrs. Tredoni's hate-lanced eyes boring into hers, then turned back to the altar.

Father Pat knelt to adore the Blood of Christ. Rising, he elevated the chalice, and the bells chimed celebration.

Father Tom entered the church from the sacristy on one side of the altar, and slowly walked up the center aisle, casually scanning the congregation.

Mrs. Tredoni watched him through narrowed lids as he came closer.

Tom saw her but looked away as he passed, then moved deliberately to the exit; not swiftening his pace until he reached the lobby.

Outside, two patrol cars blocked off the street, and a number of uniformed policemen stood with Beame and Spina. Tom rushed down the steps and ran to them.

"She's in there. Are you sure she's the one? Mrs. Tredoni's been . . ."

"We got a positive I.D. from Alphonso. Let's go get her," Spina grunted.

Tom stepped in front of him, arms outstretched. "Wait a minute. She's too close to Catherine and Alice. If she sees you, who knows what she'll do!"

Father Tom looked at Beame. "Look, it's almost time for communion. Come with me to the sacristy. When she comes up to receive, I know I can get her to go with you."

"What happens if she doesn't come up?" Spina demanded.

"Look, I know her. She'll come up. She's never missed a Sunday."

Spina gave Beame a shrewd smile. "Why can't we put a marksman in the balcony?"

"Not in my church," Tom said flatly. "I can handle her. She wouldn't do anything to me."

Beame looked from Tom to Spina. "I want men covering all the exits," he said after a moment's deliberation. "Keep out of sight. Let's go, Father."

Spina shrugged as he watched them run to the side entrance. He really hadn't expected the captain to buy his marksman idea. After this morning, all he could sell Beame was his badge.

"All right, you men," Spina yelled, waving his arms. "Fan out. If this one gets away, you're all civilians by midnight."

✠ ✠ ✠

From the door of the sacristy, Beame had a clear fix on Mrs. Tredoni.

Father Pat genuflected before the altar and began a low droning prayer.

"Panem caelestem accipiam; et nomen Dominus invocabo."

He raised his voice slightly.

"Dominus non sum dignus."

After receiving the host, Father Pat began gathering the fragments in preparation for communion—the joyous sacrifice that was the essence of the mass.

As the children in the front section filed from their pews, the center aisle behind them filled with parishioners.

Catherine rose and eased out of her pew. She leaned forward to excuse herself, and the gold crucifix swung free, searing Mrs. Tredoni's brain like a fiery sword.

Unconsciously, her fingers stroked the barren space at her throat where the cross belonged. Mesmerized by the flashing glint of the cross, Mrs. Tredoni followed Catherine to the altar.

Alice saw Mrs. Tredoni shuffle after her mother, and on a curious impulse, left her pew and trailed after.

Mrs. Tredoni was only a few feet behind Catherine when she was cut off by a group of teenagers who piled out of their pews and choked the aisle.

Beame followed every move she made from the sacristy. "You were right, Father Tom. She's coming down the aisle."

Tom stepped up beside him. "I want your word that you'll give me a chance to let her come freely."

Beame pursed his lips. "Got a plan?"

"I know she'll come quietly if I can get her at the altar rail."

"Okay, Father, be careful."

Father Tom entered the altar from the rear of the sacristy and joined the kneeling altar boy.

Tom took the paten from the boy and motioned him into the sacristy. Father Pat turned to the congregation and shot Tom an astonished look.

"Later," Tom hissed.

"Ecce Agnus Dei, ecce qui tollit peccata mundi. Dominus non sum dignus . . ." Father Pat droned, nodding slightly.

The first wave of parishioners were already kneeling at the rail. The others waited behind them, lined up on both sides of the center aisle. As Tom followed Father Pat to the right side of the altar, he focused on Catherine standing a few yards away.

Mrs. Tredoni was behind her, separated by seven or eight parishioners. Tom was relieved by the wide barrier between them until he spotted Alice.

The little girl was no more than three feet away from Mrs. Tredoni, watching her intently.

Tom kept his eye on them as Father Pat dispensed the Host in the traditional order, from right to left.

The procedure was repeated for each individual: Tom would slide the tray beneath the communicant's chin while Father Pat dipped his consecrated fingers into the chalice for the Host.

After making the sign of the cross with the small white wafer and intoning the benediction, Father Pat deposited the wafer on the communicant's tongue.

As each parishioner rose, another took his place at the rail.

Catherine approached the rail, deep in meditative prayer, and Tom saw Mrs. Tredoni pushing her way to the front of the line. Her face was shiny with perspiration as she maneuvered for a place next to Catherine.

"Hurry, Pat," he whispered urgently.

Bewildered, Father Pat rushed his prayers, fingers dipping rapidly into the chalice as he dispensed the Host, and moved on.

As Catherine knelt at the rail, Mrs. Tredoni scurried for the open space beside her.

Before she made it, Alice squeezed between, forcing Mrs. Tredoni away from her mother.

When Father Pat gave Catherine the Host, Tom tensed, ready for a sudden attack.

Father Pat moved on, but Tom waited as Catherine bowed her head in thanksgiving, his body still shielding her from harm.

Confused, Father Pat drew back.

Mrs. Tredoni remained kneeling, as Catherine left the rail. Her eyes were closed and her tongue was extended for the sacrament.

Alice watched Father Tom move past her.

"Mrs. Tredoni, I want you to come with me."

Her eyes clicked open like a mechanical bird.

"I want communion, Father," she whimpered.

"I can't give it to you now, Mrs. Tredoni. I promised them you'd come with me."

Mrs. Tredoni's hawk glare darted to Beame emerging from the sacristy, then swooped back to Father Tom. She slowly rose to her feet, shopping bag clasped in her arms.

"You gave it to that whore!" she screeched, her limbs spastic with fury.

In that moment she understood why she'd been visited by St. Michael. He'd come to tell her that the saint was no more, like the monsignor. Father Tom's soul was possessed, and she'd been chosen to save him from eternal torment.

"Please come with me . . ."

Mrs. Tredoni's hand flicked out of the shopping bag and slashed the knife across his groin like a silver whip. As Father Tom fell across the rail, she drove the heavy blade into the side of his neck, then caught his sagging weight in her arms.

She embraced him joyfully, rocking his convulsing flesh against her, crooning softly amid the screams as life bubbled from his lips in frothy red gobs.

Alice's bulging eyes registered a splintered sequence of images through the rolling confusion.

Father Pat dropped the chalice, and the wafers spilled across the carpet. Moaning loudly, he crawled across the floor to retrieve them.

Detective Spina ran down the center aisle with a gun, pushing everyone aside.

Captain Beame tried to pull Mrs. Tredoni away from Father Tom, but she clutched him tightly; laughing and praying as blood gushed from both sides of the knife jutting from his neck.

Catherine was tearing at her hair and kicking at the people trying to hold her.

After they led Mrs. Tredoni away, no one saw Alice creep forward and pick up the knife from the floor except for Father Tom. He lay at the base of the altar rail, watching with unblinking amazement as she reached for the shopping bag nearby and peered inside. She studied the mask, veil, and other things it contained for a long time before tenderly placing the blood-oiled blade beside them.

Then her gaze lifted over the milling throng around her and floated toward the dazzling shimmer outside, as if seeing the world for the first time.